GENUINE SWEET

GENUINE SWEET

Faith Harkey

Houghton Mifflin Harcourt
Boston   New York

For information about permission to reproduce selections from this book,
write to Permissions, Houghton Mifflin Harcourt Publishing Company,
3 Park Avenue, 19th Floor, New York, New York 10016.

The text was set in in Carre Noir Std.

www.hmhco.com

The Library of Congress has cataloged the hardcover edition as follows:

Harkey, Faith.

Genuine Sweet/Faith Harkey.

p. cm.

Summary: Genuine Sweet, twelve, of tiny, impoverished Sass, Georgia, inherited
the ability to grant any wish except her own but with help from new friends, her life
and town are improving until unexpected trouble arrives and Genuine learns the
difference between wishing for a better life and building one.

[1. Wishes—Fiction. 2. Magic—Fiction. 3. Family life—Georgia—Fiction. 4.
Community life—Georgia—Fiction. 5. Georgia—Fiction.] I. Title.

PZ7.1.H37Gen2015

[Fic]—dc23 2014027739

ISBN: 978-0-544-28366-4 hardcover

ISBN: 978-0-544-66853-9 paperback

Manufactured in the United States of America
DOC 10 9 8 7 6 5 4 3 2 1
4500583144

For the joy of it—

CONTENTS

1

FIRST HELPING

GENUINE SWEET. THAT'S ME. AND SINCE EVERYONE always asks how I came by such an unlikely name, I might as well tell you now.

Twelve years ago, on a night so dark the midwife couldn't find her way through the woods to our house, my ma gave birth to me. They say it was a long labor, and a hard one, and her body just tuckered out, so she died. But before she died, Ma held me in her arms and looked down at me and smiled.

"She's a genuine treasure," Ma said.

Pa, whose family name is Sweet, was only slightly drunk when he added, "Ten fingers, ten toes, and ugly as get-out. A genuine Sweet."

Gram swatted Pa on the head and told him to hush. "All newborns are a little soggy. They've been floating in goo for nine months." Turning to Ma, she asked, "What'll you call her, Cristabel?"

Ma glanced at Pa, who she loved very much even though he was dumb as a post when he drank, which was most of the time. "Genuine Sweet. Genuine Beauty Sweet."

I usually don't tell people about the "Beauty" part because, as you can see, I'm not one. Big buckteeth and more freckles than you'll find stars in a backwoods sky. But you don't seem like the teasing sort, and besides, you say you're here to know the whole story, and I believe you.

I guess the other thing you'll want to hear about is how I came to be in such an unusual line of work. There aren't a whole lot of twelve-year-old wish fetchers, and even fewer who end up in a muddle like mine. So here's the truth, plain and simple. My gram used to say this, by the way. I never take credit where it's not due. She said, *Necessity is the mother of invention.*

See, in small towns like Sass, Georgia, towns where one logging company employs three-quarters of the citizenry, you don't find a whole lot of fresh opportunity. So when Pa Sweet showed up drunk to work one day and nearly cut off Bill Hasting's right hand with the circular saw, there weren't too many other jobs for him to choose from. He did apply for the part-time security opening at the old folks' home, but as you might imagine, no one was too pleased with the idea of leaving the safety of all those seniors to Dangerous Dale Sweet, as he'd come to be called.

Me and Pa were broke. Gram kicked in as much as she

could from her Social Security check, and moved in with us to help make ends meet, but in the end, we were hungry most of the time, and even chubby Gram was starting to look a little pinched.

One night, as I lay in bed, my stomach rumbling something fierce, I tried to think of an idea, anything to bring in a little extra cash. I was no scholar, so a career in tutoring the younger kids was probably out. And as for babysitting, who would ever hire Dangerous Dale Sweet's daughter?

About then, I started thinking of Gram's vanilla spice cake, which, if you like sweets, I won't let you leave without the recipe for it. It's light and heavy all at once, just the thing to fill up an empty and—I'll say it—forlorn-feeling belly. So, there I was, thinking about that cake. With a glass of milk on the side. Warm milk, maybe, with a sprinkling of nutmeg on top—and all of the sudden I remembered something.

It had been some months prior, a few days after my last birthday, before Pa lost his job. Gram and I had been snacking on leftover vanilla spice cake, which still had holes in it from where my twelve candles had gone.

"Now that you've come to your womanhood, there's something you ought to know," Gram had said.

I set down my fork to listen. As I mentioned, this was before we got to be so hungry that not even a black bear could have come between me and a piece of cake.

Gram reached into the pocket of her apron and pulled out

a yellowed piece of newspaper. She unfolded it gingerly, so it wouldn't tear. The headline read, MACINTYRE GIRL GRANTS BOY'S LAST WISH. "That's Flo MacIntyre, my mama, your great-gram."

I read the short clipping. It mentioned a crowd of people gathering to watch Great-Gram MacIntyre sing to the stars, which, somehow, had something to do with a sick boy who'd died happy.

I shrugged at Gram, baffled.

"You and me," Gram began slowly, "and your ma, too—all of us MacIntyre women—we're wish fetchers." The way she said it, I could tell she felt she'd offered me the keys to a real treasure chest.

"Really?" I said, trying to rally some excitement. I knew I'd failed, so I went ahead and admitted, "I don't, uh, I don't know what that is."

"No. No, I reckon you wouldn't." She used her tongue to fiddle with her dentures. "All right. Think of it this way. Some folks are born knowing how to play the guitar. The first time you set the box in their hands, they can play you a tune. Right?"

I nodded.

"And some people can crochet a doily like nobody's business. Your great-great-uncle Felix was that way, Lord bless him." She folded the clipping and set it back in her pocket.

"The women in our family, we have a certain shine, too. We can draw down the magic from the stars. We can grant wishes."

"Like the genie in the bottle?" I asked with a little laugh because, truth to tell, I didn't believe a word of it.

But she kept on.

"A genie is a made-up thing, an old story. Besides, genies were always trying to trick people," said Gram. "Wish fetchers are real. The underlings of angels, my ma used to say, with humbler clothes."

We didn't say much more about it then. It had been a nice story, I figured, but not much more than that, and surely Gram had been able to tell I hadn't been in a snake-oil kind of mood that night.

So, as I said, that's what I was thinking of on that hungry, hungry night some months ago. Vanilla spice cake and the clabberheaded notion that I might have wish fetching in my blood. Foolish, really.

Of course, I'd never known Gram to lie . . .

And we were a fourth-generation *Sass* family, after all. The town was full of folks who had family shines. Everyone knew Mina Cunningham was a pain lifter and the Fullers could soothe bad dreams. But granting wishes? That was hanging the basket mighty high.

Just then, a mouse so familiar I'd named it Scooter skittered across the floor. Our house had more cracks than it did walls. It wasn't bad enough we were hungry. Winter was coming, and without money to pay the electric, we'd soon be cold. Dangerous cold. I was *scared*.

But wishes—that would remedy everything. Not just now, but forever.

All right, then. I'd play the huckleberry. But what should I wish *for?* At first, I wasn't sure. Maybe for my pa to wake up and get sober and fix things before they broke any worse. Not real likely. There was a better chance of my dead ma showing up at the door with angel's wings and a basket of money.

Hmm.

Food. House repairs. Electricity through the winter. All the things we needed. It pretty much came down to cash.

Simple enough, I figured.

Now. How would a body go about fetching a wish? In the end, I couldn't think of any other way but to say it out loud.

I took a deep breath. In the moment before I spoke, my belly lurched. First, because my wish might actually come true. Second, because I knew it probably would not.

I wish, I wish—*oh, please*—*I wish . . .*

"I wish-fetch myself one thousand dollars!" I spoke into the night.

I know what you're thinking. Why only a thousand? But I reckoned if I really was a wish fetcher, I could always wish up some more. Better to start small.

The amount ended up not mattering a whit. I could have wished for a million. The outcome would have been the same.

Nothing happened.

But remember, now, I was desperate. There was no way I was going to give up after the first try.

No, what I needed was a little schooling.

I got up out of my bed—which was the living room sofa—and went into Gram's room—which used to be my old room.

"You sleeping, Gram?" I whispered.

Gram's dentures clacked. "Who'sit! Who'sit!"

"Shht. Gram. It's just me." I sparked a match and lit the candle beside her bed. "I need to ask you something."

"You scared the golly out of me!" Her face looked a little green in the candlelight.

"Sorry. Didn't mean to."

"Well, what is it?" Gram sat up in the grumpiest manner she could muster.

"Do you think . . ." I looked at the flickering of the little candle flame.

"Yeah?"

My stomach rumbled. I stuck my fist in my gut to shush it. "Did you mean what you said, after my birthday, about all that wish-granting stuff?"

Gram blinked. "I did. I do."

I nodded, chewing on that. "Do you think you might teach me to grant wishes?"

She smiled just a little. "I think I could."

"And then I could wish us a better life? With money and food and all?"

"Ah," she sighed. "I see."

"What? What's wrong?"

"A wish fetcher can't grant their own wishes, Gen," she replied.

I pondered that for a while.

"Well, you can do it, too, right? What if you grant me and I'll grant you and we can both of us grant Pa? He could use a double dose of wish, surely."

She shook her head. "Can't."

I flared my nostrils. There's few things that bother me as much as a person who gives up easily. "Gram, you are hungry, ain't you?"

A pause. "Yes."

"You wanna be hungry any longer than you absolutely have to be?" I asked.

Just then, her belly made a sound like an angry cat.

"No," Gram admitted.

"Then shouldn't we at least *try?*"

She thought this over.

"Lemme tell you a true story." She wrapped a blanket around my shoulders.

"A mess of years ago," she said, "there was a man, a wish fetcher who lived in the city of Fenn. It was a big city, one of the grandest in all the South, mostly because of this man, who spent his days granting the good-hearted wishes of the people." She pointed a finger at me. "*Good-hearted wishes.* Let that be the only kind you ever fetch, you mark me?"

I nodded.

"So, here's this man," Gram went on, "granting wishes. And one day he wakes up and realizes everyone in Fenn is getting everything they want—except him! He'd fetched wishes for loving wives and housefuls of kids, good jobs and good health, and what did he ever get from it? He lived comfortably enough, sure, but *he* had no wife, no kids, no job but granting wishes, and, sure as sunshine, he came down with a bad cold every August, no matter what."

"See! That's just what I mean!" I interrupted. "Why couldn't he grant his own wishes? Nothing bad, just good things."

Gram held up a finger. "But he *did*. He broke the wish fetcher's first rule and wished himself a wife and two apple-cheeked young'uns. And they were happy, and he went on granting wishes for other people, too. But then his tub sprang a leak, and it was all too easy to fetch a wish to fix it. And when his oldest daughter started to turn fat, it was easier to grant her beauty than it was to teach her to eat right. Wishes and wishes, faster and faster they came, until his whole life was built on wishes, and he wasn't fetching any for anyone else."

"But I wouldn't—" I blurted.

"He never thought he would, either," Gram said. "One day, he had a fight with the mayor, and it suddenly seemed to make ever so much sense just to wish *himself* mayor. Another day, when the egg lady's chickens stopped laying due to cold, rather than wait for warmer weather along with everyone else, he wished up his own eggs, and started to sell those, too. Afore you know it, the chicken lady was out of business. Soon, the man wasn't just the mayor, he was the boss of the whole town. He sold the best of everything, because he didn't have to fashion it or grow it or even give it much more than a thought—he only had to wish it up. And people *loved him*."

Gram crinkled her eyes. "And they *hated him*. Resented him. You know what that means?"

I nodded.

"Even his wife and kids started to resent him because they thought he should fetch them the skill to grant wishes, too. Why do you think he didn't?" Gram asked.

"So he'd be the only boss?" I replied.

"I think so." She was quiet for a time. "In the end, he died suddenly, and the whole town was ruined because nobody remembered how to grow crops or raise chickens or hammer iron. People went hungry or had to move away to cities where they could buy things other people still knew how to make. Fenn became a ghost town. And the man, his name was cursed for all time."

I considered Gram's story. "It doesn't have to turn out that way."

She gave me a fierce look. "Maybe not, but you heed this, Gen Sweet. *Them what breaks that rule pays a price.* Unless you promise to never, ever fetch your own wishes — or talk other people into asking for things you want for yourself — I won't teach you diddly. You understand?"

I understood.

"But what good does it do to grant other people's wishes when we're starving?" I demanded.

"Good given away always comes back to you, Gen. Don't you know that by now?" she asked.

"So, you're saying that if I do good things, I'll get good things?"

"Yes, but that's not why you do them —"

"Gram!" I whisper-hollered. "We got to do something! Spend winter in *this* house? With hardly any food and no heat? We could *die!*"

Gram gave a little nod. "I guess we could."

I could feel my eyes bulging. "Well, then?"

She folded her hands in her lap and seemed to be thinking hard.

"All right. Let's see if we can nudge the Lord just a little," she agreed. "Never hurts to do a good deed, anyway."

2

WITH HUMBLER CLOTHES

W E PASSED PA, WHO'D FALLEN ASLEEP SITTING up on an apple crate on the front porch. He reeked of drink, and I wondered, not for the first or the fortieth time, how he'd paid for it.

Gram waved me on into the woods, her slippers making a *hush-hush* sound as she shuffled over the ground, a bed of fallen and decaying leaves. The air smelled of night and damp and good woods—sort of musty and peaceful, if a smell can be peaceful, which I think it can.

She led me to a clearing, a spot not too far from Squirrel Tail Creek, a place where I'd sometimes come to watch the critters come and go. In the city, I hear all you've got are stray cats and dogs and pigeons, but in Sass, we have bear and deer and coyote, plus the cows and horses, if you count them, though they're not wild.

Gram took two nested plastic cups from the pocket of her robe and gave me one.

"Now, to grant a wish, you've got to draw the magic from the stars," Gram said. "For that, you'll need a cup and a good, solid whistle."

"Like a pennywhistle?"

She waved a hand. "Not unless it's so cold your lips don't work right. No, all's you have to do is blow, loud and clear." She pursed her lips and let out an impressive trill.

"I didn't know you could do that." I laughed.

"It's in the blood." She smiled. "You try."

Let me tell you, there are some champion whistlers at school—you mostly hear it in the grades where the girls are wearing bras—but me, I've always been more of a screamer if I wanted to get someone's attention. Still, I gave it my best try.

It must have been all right, because Gram nodded. "Good. Now, all's you have to do is whistle like that and hold out your cup this way."

Gram held her cup in both hands and lifted it up to the sky. She trilled again.

I couldn't help feeling she did look like an angel, just then, in her long white bathrobe, her white hair falling loose around her shoulders, every part of her—even her teeth, 'cause she smiled—glowing in the starlight.

"Y'all come now. Come on," she crooned, and whistled again.

I was about to register my opinion that this was all starting to feel a little foolish, when the light of one of the brighter stars seemed to shine a little brighter still. I looked at it, really concentrating on it, and tried to make out if I was seeing things. After a time, though, there was no denying it. The beams that radiated from that star turned more liquid than light and began to pour down from the sky. Something very like quicksilver, it fell in soft rivulets that poured right into Gram's cup, just as if she held it under the faucet of heaven.

Gram waited for the last of the silver to dribble into her cup, then held it out for me to look. If you can imagine silver water that smells like carnations, that's pretty much how it seemed to me.

"Pure starlight," Gram said reverently.

"Do you drink it?" I asked.

"My ma did," she replied. "And all the words she spoke for the next day turned true. But me, I use it to water seeds."

Gram reached into her pocket and pulled out a bit of lint. "Just today, Roxanne Fuller was telling me she wished she had enough gas in her car to go visit her grandkids. 'One tank'd do it, to get me there and back,' she said. Now, just because someone wants something doesn't mean you belt out a whistle and fetch it right up. You got to take care. But Roxie's my best friend, and when a friend says a thing like that, all sad and desperate, what can you do but lend a hand?"

She took the lint between her finger and thumb and rolled it into a tight ball. "One full tank of gas for Roxanne Fuller."

Then, with a spoon she pulled from her pocket, she dug a little hole and planted her seed. Once she'd covered it with earth, she poured the starlight over it, much in the way a person would water a plant.

"Grow," she told it. "Grow."

Gram put the cup and spoon back in her pocket, brushed off her hands, and said, "That's all there is to it."

"And now Missus Fuller has a full tank of gas?" I asked.

"I reckon she will."

"Nuh-uh!" I didn't say it because I didn't believe her, exactly. But you know, it was just such a crazy, incredible claim, and I guess a body feels obligated to protest in moments like that.

"Yuh-huh." She grinned. "Tomorrow morning, you go see."

"All right, I will."

"And collect yourself a wish or two," said Gram. "People don't have to know you're doing it. Truth to tell, it's probably best that they don't. Just give an ear to folks' hopes and needs. Then, tomorrow night, whistle you down some magic. Mm?"

The next day, I did just as Gram had told me. I snuck out past Pa, who was still snoring on the porch, and left for Missus Fuller's.

I think I like Sass best in the mornings while Main Street's still empty and the stores are all dark. This place has been around since before the Civil War — some of the buildings are just that old — and when there's no cars or folks around, I imagine Gram's gram walking along, doing her errands, wearing one of those fancy, old-time dresses and maybe a pair of dainty gloves with ruffles at the wrists.

The trees are even older than the buildings, so *they* would have seen Gram's gram directly, and she would have seen them, too. It comforts me somehow — even though I'll never get to look her in the eye, precisely, I can lay my hand on the very same tree she might have taken shade under on a summer day.

I greeted the trees with a nod, and the squirrels, too, who chittered as I passed by. I'm a little crazy like that, talking to things that can't talk back, and I'm not ashamed to admit it. Besides, truth is, maybe they do talk back and we're just not smart enough to understand them.

Missus Fuller's home was just a block past Main, a big

old place that used to be a popular boarding house, run by her ma and pa. My own gram had lived there for a number of years, until she moved in with Pa and me. It was mostly empty now, except for the occasional drifter who rented a room passing through on their way to someplace else.

I found Missus Fuller sitting on her porch, a mug in hand, watching the steam rise from her coffee. I thought she looked a little lonesome.

"Morning, Missus Fuller," I called from her gate.

"Gen-u-wine Sweet!" She waved a beckoning hand. "Come in! Come in!"

Missus Fuller felt beside her chair for her cane and gingerly pushed herself upright. Not much older than Gram, she colored her hair a soft pinkish-red color, which I always thought gave her a bright appearance.

"You're just in time!" She opened her front door, stepped in, and said over her shoulder, "Fresh blueberry muffins cooling on the stove!"

"Don't trouble yourself, ma'am," I called, but secretly I was delighted at the thought of something other than mush for breakfast.

"Trouble!" She laughed as I stepped into her kitchen. I don't think there was a single spoon, plate, or butter dish without a picture of a chicken on it. "A muffin's for eating. There's no trouble in that. Sit."

Missus Fuller beamed as I devoured two muffins and a

tall glass of orange juice. The berries were so fat and juicy, the blue-tinged cake so sweet, I nearly forgot why I'd come.

Eventually, though, it did come back to me, and as I set my empty glass on the table, I said, "I was wondering, Missus Fuller, if you could do something for me."

She blinked placidly at me. "Sure, honey."

"I don't know how to say this, exactly, but my gram and I were talking last night and your situation came up—about how you wished for a tank of gas so you could visit your grandkids."

Missus Fuller nodded.

"And, well, we thought there might be something we could do about that, and so we . . . wished on a star, I guess, that you might have your tank of gas, seeing as how it would make you so happy to see your kin."

Missus Fuller got a funny look then—well, two funny looks. The first one was the kind of face a person might make when someone asks them to donate money and they don't want to. But the second look was something else, as if she was secretly not an old lady at all, but a little girl in an old body. The second look won out.

Her eyes shone and she gave a mischievous sort of grin. "Let's look."

The two of us got up from the table, the legs of our chairs scraping the floor loudly. We hustled out to her garage, where her long white Cadillac, older than me, sat quietly.

Missus Fuller opened the car door and handed me her cane. "The best way's to start it up, so we can see for real how much gas is in it."

She eased herself into the driver's seat and put the key in the ignition. The car grumbled before it roared, and—just a quick tick later—that little girl inside Missus Fuller was hooting and clapping her hands and bouncing around.

"Hooo!" was all she could say for a time, but eventually she did manage the words, "Full tank! Full tank! Baby girls, here I come!"

What do you do with something like this, I ask you? What do you do when you wake up one day and realize pigs just might fly, for real? As for me, I did the strangest thing. I broke down and cried.

I guess it was because I remembered right then that my ma was dead, my daddy was a drunk, and this morning's blueberry muffins were the first time I'd felt full up in a season. Why hadn't someone fetched a wish for me? For my ma? It hurt my heart to think about how easy it had been to wish up that tank of gas, especially when I considered everything that went into drilling oil and refining it, shipping it 'cross the country in trucks—all the people and all the effort: so gigantic! Somehow, the magic in the stars had swept aside all those details in some special way to fill up Missus Fuller's car. Couldn't somebody get out their broom on my behalf?

"Genuine, are you all right?" Missus Fuller asked. "Honey, what is it?"

Her eyes were so bright and her happiness was so real, I just couldn't ruin it with my complaining.

"I'm glad for you, is all," I said.

She gave me a big hug and laughed from her belly. "Sometimes life surprises you, don't it?" She set her hands on the steering wheel as if she was ready to drive off. "I guess I should pack a few things. Can you wait a minute? I'll give you a ride home. It's on my way."

I squinched my nose. "Naw, thanks. I like to walk. Plus, I've got some other errands."

"If you're sure," Missus Fuller said. "You thank your granny for me, all right, Genuine? That was a mighty nice thing, considering—well, seeing as how—I just know that was a difficult thing for her to do, after all this time."

I was in a sort of daze when I left Missus Fuller, so I wandered for a time, until I came to a tree whose branches dipped down like the streams of a fountain. I sat butt to dirt and leaned my head back against the trunk. The tree felt sturdy and alive, and I liked thinking of the idea that it breathed my air while I breathed its. Before long, I felt mostly better. After all, it had been a mighty right thing, to be able to make Missus Fuller smile that way. Even if *my* life didn't change, if I really could help folks, wasn't that better than nobody's life changing, nobody smiling new smiles? If I couldn't smile for me, I'd smile for them. That was that.

And for a time, that *was* that. But I'm no angel. It's easy to be glad for others' happiness *sometimes*. But *all* the time? Even on your worst days, your hurting days? That's the hard part. You'll see what I mean when I come to the part of the story where—well, you'll see.

I got up, dusted myself off, and tried to think of someplace somebody might be wishing something. Three things came to me: the ball field, the old folks' home, and the hospital. I decided against the ball field, because anyone wishing for a home run couldn't wait until nighttime for me to whistle down the magic. As for the nursing home, my ma had been the cleaning girl there, and since no one ever quits a job in Sass, there's plenty of people on staff who remember her real well and always find it necessary to say so. Maybe I'd go there on a day when my tears weren't quite so close to hand.

Instead, I drifted down Main Street, passing a dozen or so faces I knew almost as well as my own. My feet carried me past Ham's Diner, the drugstore, and our few empty storefronts, beyond the city hall, then finally toward the hospital.

Now, you, coming from the city, might not think too much of our tiny town. Our stores, by and large, open at nine and close at six. The barber, playing the banjo on the bench outside his shop, may seem downright provincial to your eye. But small-town life can be a mighty fine thing when you're hurt and needing comfort.

For instance, consider Nurse Cussler, who was tacking a flyer to the town bulletin board. Two years back, when I broke my arm, she was there. When the doc was about to set my bone, Nurse Cussler got me talking about the gorge. So there we were, saying how fall was coming and how the leaves would change and the whole gorge would turn into a vision of apricot and gold and—*sitch!*—that's when the doc set my arm. Of course it hurt, but I know it didn't hurt as bad as it could have, and I can't help thinking that all that talk of sunlight shining through autumn leaves somehow gave me the heart to heal up fast and well, which I did.

I glanced over to read the flyer Nurse Cussler had posted. A charity benefit for Mister Apfel, who needed important medical treatment and couldn't pay for it.

Hmm.

Probably, there wasn't a soul in Sass who *didn't* have *some* kind of wish. Only yesterday, Nurse Cussler had told me that Greg Mittler was in the hospital with his whole face swole up. (*Anaphylactic shock*, she had whispered confidentially.) Surely Greg wished that whole catastroke would just disappear! And I knew for a fact that Ham had been longing for a new freezer for a couple years now. These were important, real things my neighbors needed. And here I was, maybe, with the gift of fetching 'em for them. How could I pick?

Hands in my pockets, I stood on the street corner, thinking it over.

Just down the way, Edie Walton flipped the OPEN sign on the community college's outreach office door, where she was both a worker and a scholar. Jeb Turner's truck pulled between two rows of rental storage units, passing a sign that pointed to a highway that would take a person into the distant, summer-green mountains.

A few paces off, out front of Marvin's Hunt Shop and Prom Gear, a girl about my own age held a cell phone up to the sky. If she was looking for a connection, she wouldn't find it there. The *only* spot cell phones worked in Sass was from atop the roof of Ham's Diner. Since the girl plainly didn't know that—and since I knew neither her name nor her face—she was plainly a stranger. Which in Sass was quite a rarity.

Looking lost *and* far away from home?

"Maybe she's needing a wish," I reasoned, and started across the street.

The girl was truly beautiful, with brown skin the color of chestnuts, long eyelashes, and a quality I guess the beauty-pageant people might call grace—even though she was only standing there contemplating her phone. In fact, everything about her was pageant-pretty. And here was me, plain little Genuine. I was embarrassed just to be walking toward her. Maybe I'd go see if poor, swollen Greg over at the hospital could mumble a wish.

"Hi! Excuse me!" the stranger called out, just as I was turning away. "Could you tell me how to get to the library?"

Determined not to let my uneasiness affect my manners, I smiled. "Sure!"

"I've been trying all over the place, but I can't get a signal," she said, holding up her phone. "Would they have Internet at the library?"

I walked on over. "You're not from around here!"

You may have heard this greeting and wondered at it. We really do mean it to be friendly.

She stood stock-still for a time, and I thought I might have offended her. Then she bit her lip on one side and stuck her tongue out the other. "How could you tell?"

I couldn't help laughing at that.

She held out one manicured hand and said, "Jura Carver. Ardenville refugee."

Ardenville, if you're not familiar with it, is the closest big city. It's known mainly for its eight-lane highways and its many aluminum-chair manufactories.

I took her hand and gave it a shake. "Genuine Sweet." Feeling pressed to add my own little something of interest, I tacked on, "Wish fetcher."

Jura jerked her chin back. "Wish fetcher? What's that?"

I found myself wondering just then if it was a good idea, telling folks about my wishing. Missus Fuller's expression had been downright peculiar when I'd told her what Gram and me had been up to. But all of the sudden, I *really* needed to talk about that full tank of gas and the rest of my wish-fetching puzzlement. And it seemed a lot easier to tell it to a stranger, someone I'd never, ever see again, than to talk to someone who already knew me as Dangerous Dale Sweet's daughter.

And so, on a whim some might consider foolish, I set the whole ball of wax before her. Fourth-generation, no selfish wishes, starlight pouring from the sky. Everything. And I was real glad to get it off my chest.

Until Jura gave me her own peculiar expression—part stare, part lime-pucker.

"Hmm," was all she said.

Seconds ticked by.

I could feel the red rising to my cheeks. I'd cut the fool, and that was all there was to it.

"But *you* wanted the library, ha-ha!" I nearly shouted. Jura took a shocked half-step backward. "Which is *right* across the street from my second cousin's beauty shop. Her name's Faye, so's you know. She's real, real good at hair. And she's got a library card. Pretty much everyone does. Which is why it's *so* easy to find!" I giggled, giddy with embarrassment. "All in one building! City hall, the police department, the library, the extension office. Even the historical society, should you have the need."

"A need for a historical society?" Jura asked.

"You never know." I grinned tightly.

Jura looked where I was pointing, then turned her gaze my way.

"A wish fetcher?" she asked.

". . . Yep."

"And this liquid light you're talking about, it's really from the stars? Sort of a . . . quantum fruit punch?"

I didn't understand that, precisely, but my gut told me we were on the same page. "Sure!"

She thought about that. "Sounds sort of like a water witch. You know, the way the talent runs in families?"

"A water witch?" I tried to remember what that was. "Like a dowser?"

She nodded. "My great-grandma was one. Only, I don't think I can do it. I tried once, right over one of the city water mains, and my stick didn't so much as twitch," Jura admitted. "But still, I believe people *can* do it."

"Oh, surely, so do I. The McCleans, up on Stotes Hill, are known for it," I said. "You should try your dowsing here. Amy McClean says the ley lines are real strong in Sass."

"Ley lines are places where *power* collects," Jura mused. She gave me a long, careful look and said, "Wishes, huh?"

I nodded.

She broke into a smile — a beautiful one, of course. "That's cool, Genuine." Even though she was from the city, she pronounced it right: Gen-u-wine.

"So, what are you going to do with it?" she asked, heading for the library.

"I was just studying on that. I don't rightly know," I said, walking alongside her.

"Think of all the good you could do!" Her eyes got bright and wide. "I mean, you could stop war! House the homeless!"

My stomach rumbled. "Feed the hungry."

"Exactly!"

Then came one of those moments, the sort where two people run out of things to say and they end up staring at their shoes. Seeing as how I knew everybody in Sass, it had been years since I'd made anything resembling a new friend. I wasn't sure I recalled how to do it. I cast about for something to say.

"I live just past Jackrabbit Bend," I blurted. "If you need help finding the post office or something."

"Thanks." She bobbed her head. "If I get to stay, I may take you up on that."

That got my attention. "You might be staying?"

"I hope so. I want to. Even though I'm going crazy with

nothing but staticky news and the cooking channel! How do you stand it with only two stations?"

I laughed. "You stay in Sass long enough, you'll get used to making do. The older kids even made up a cooking-channel drinking game."

"What do they drink?" Jura asked, a mite scandalized. "Moonshine or something?"

"Naw. Just milk. We've got a lot of it around here. Cow and goat and even sheep—"

"Sheep!"

"I don't think anybody's made moonshine here since Prohibition days," I went on. "It's easy enough to go to Chippy's, if you're a drinker." I frowned and changed the subject. "Not too many people move to Sass. Does your family work for the lumber mill or something?"

She shook her head. "My auntie lives here. You know Trish Spencer?"

I told her I did. Miz Spencer was the manager of the credit union.

"Well," Jura continued, "my mom and I were thinking could I stay with her so I could get away from my old vomitorium of a school. But it turns out I probably can't because my aunt's not my legal guardian, blah, blah, blah."

"Your school's real bad?" I asked.

Her eyes darted after a crow that flew by. "You must've

heard *something* about big-city schools, even on your staticky news channel. Metal detectors in the halls. Locker searches."

"I can see how that might lick the red off your candy," I said. "So, your parents can't move here?"

"Parent. Singular." She shook her head. "And no, my mom can't move here unless she gets a job, which she can't, 'cause there aren't any."

"Tell me about it," I replied, trying not to think too much about Pa.

And then I came to it. Right in front of me, I had the raw makings of a wish! All it needed was a little patting and baking. "So, uh, Jura. If you had your druthers—"

"My *what?*"

I wasn't offended. It wasn't Jura's fault she came from the city, where folks' talk was dry as sawdust. "You know, your pick. If you had your pick," I clarified.

"Oh."

"What would you choose?" I continued. "For your auntie to be your guardian or your ma to get a job here?"

Jura lit up. "Oh, my mom to get a job, definitely! She hates Ardenville! She'd be so happy. And Auntie, too, she'd practically be dancing around with a rose between her teeth—"

I imagined Sass's prim and proper banker, Trish Spencer, turning a tango 'round her living room, and I began to cackle. "Nuh-unh!"

The notion must have struck Jura funny, too, because there she was, giggling right along with me.

After a time, Jura wiped the mirth water from her eyes. "You're thinking about wish fetching it, aren't you? For me and my mom?"

"Unless you don't want me to," I told her.

"Really? You'd use your first wish on two strangers?"

I nodded.

"Live here. In Sass. For real." Jura considered the Sass Police ATV as it rumbled by. She watched Davy Pierce leading Curly, his 4-H sheep, on a leash down Main Street.

At last, she took a deep breath and said, "If you *really* want to do this for me, Genuine, then yes! Two channels and no cell phone reception is a small price to pay to get away from those drones at Ardenville Central Middle. Ha! Even that name is stupid!"

I chuckled.

Jura put her phone in her purse. "And you know what? If you need some help with the whole wish-to-save-the-world, relief-of-human-suffering thing, I'm totally in," she said.

"Deal." We shook on it.

"I'll let you get to the library, then," I said. "I should warn you, though, it's only itty-bitty."

"Are there computers?" she asked.

"Two of 'em."

"That's all I need."

We stopped outside the city hall.

"All right, Miss Jura." I set my hands on my hips. "Meet me here tomorrow morning, and we'll see what I can do."

There we parted ways. Jura to her computer, and me to consider two things: my first, real-live wish, and Jura's notion of wishing to save the world.

3

MIRACLE FLOUR

ON MY WAY HOME, DILLY BARKER FLAGGED ME down and handed me a sack of flour for Gram.

Dilly, who was only a year or two older than my ma would have been, was the sort of neighbor who always lent a hand when troubles set in.

"Tell her somebody canceled their order, so I had extra," she said.

I told her I would and spent the rest of my walk trying to figure out a comfortable way to carry a ten-pound lumpy rectangle. Over the shoulder, under the arm—I was switching it from the crook of one elbow to the other when I came upon my own dirt road.

"Gram!" I hollered from the gate. Pa was off on a bender, so I wasn't worried about waking him. "Dilly Barker sent some flour!"

The front door swung open. Gram was dressed and made up for the day. You'd have thought she was expecting company, if it weren't for the mangy-looking fuzzy slippers on her feet. At the sight of the flour, her eyes lit up—and dimmed just as quick.

"Charity? Have we really come to that?" She clicked her tongue.

"She had a canceled order, she said."

"Hmm," Gram said skeptically, but she took the flour all the same. "Well, what do you say to dumplings and broth for lunch?"

After muffins for breakfast, it sounded sort of like a miracle, but I didn't say so.

It took a while for Gram to coax enough ingredients from our pantry to assemble a respectable meal, so while she worked, I told her about Jura and Jura's wish, and also about Greg Mittler's swollen face.

Gram frowned. "Poor boy. You hate to see something like that happen to a newcomer. He'll presume we're all bad luck."

I gave an amused shake of my head. Truth to tell, Greg had lived in Sass for at least three years, but anyone who isn't actually born here will always be "new in town."

"I think he knows us pretty well by now, Gram."

"This Jura—you say she's Trish Spencer's kin?" She wiped a smudge of flour from her nose.

I said she was.

"And you mentioned your wish fetching to her?" A look of concern crossed Gram's face.

"You didn't say it was a secret," I said.

"No, not a secret, exactly."

"Then what?"

Gram pressed her lips tight against each other. "It's just that . . . some things ain't exactly fit for public consumption, is all."

"Public consumption?" What on earth was she getting at?

Gram wiped her hands on her apron and reached for the salt shaker. She joggled it twice before she realized it was empty.

"You never know what a person might think. Or do. That's all I'm saying." She set a bowl of soup before me. "A wish fetcher has a lot of responsibility. It can be a burden for anyone—but for a young'un, especially. I kept it from your ma until she was sixteen. I probably should have waited to tell you, too." Her nostrils flared. "You ain't the only one worried about practical things, I s'pose."

I took to my soup with such vigor, broth dribbled down my chin. Gram wiped it away with her thumb.

"You know," she went on, "you might find that wish fetching is . . . specialer when the wishes come more infrequent. And without anybody knowing. Some fetchers do feel that way. Fewer wishes to pack a bigger . . . quieter wallop."

"There are other wish fetchers?" I asked, hopeful that someone might give us a leg up after all.

She looked a little disappointed. I knew why. All that stuff she'd just said, she thought I'd only heard the smallest part of it. But it wasn't true. It's just that I was homing in on the piece that mattered most. The piece that could feed us and such.

Even so, she did answer me. "So your great-gram used to tell me, though I've never met any that wasn't kin, as far as I know."

So much for that notion of a leg up.

"What kind of a wish fetcher was Ma?" I asked. "Lots of wishes or hardly any?"

"Your ma?" Gram set a soup bowl at her place and made an *ooph* noise as she sat. "She did things different. Preferred to grant the wishes of strangers. Looks like you and she might have that in common.

"Anyhow, what she'd do was put an ad in the Ardenville paper, the big one, you know? *Wishes granted,* it would say, *in exchange for good deeds.* People would write her all sorts of letters — young'uns and old folks and all in between, telling Cristabel their stories, their fears and dreams and whatnot. I still have those letters. And Cristabel would whistle to the stars for 'em and send back a little gold card she'd make with her own hands. Always said the same thing. *Your wish is granted. Please pay one good deed to a neighbor or a stranger at your earliest possible convenience.*" Gram shook her head fondly. "'At your earliest possible convenience.' She loved to talk like that, like she worked in an office. Do you know she wanted to be a secretary? Only there wasn't no call for one in town."

Hearing Gram talk about Ma that way, I couldn't help feeling proud. Wish fetching wasn't just real — it was powerful enough to touch people's hearts and change their lives. What if Jura had been right and I really could fix the world with wishes? Up till that day, I'd only ever been homely Genuine Sweet, Dangerous Dale's daughter. But what if I could be something more? What if, once I got the family fed and warm, I set about to do something really big, something only a wish fetcher could do?

Suddenly I was itching to fetch my first wish.

"So you'll come out with me tonight? Help me call down the magic from the stars?" I asked.

Gram waved a hand. "You don't need me standing over you. Better if you find your own way. Besides, I need my rest. I am an old woman, you know." She winked, but I couldn't help thinking she did look awfully tired.

I was collecting my starlight-catching cup from the cabinet when Gram mused, "Hard to say what'll upset folk. Probably best to start small and quiet, don't you think? Just because we can whistle to the stars don't mean we should try to outshine them!" Gram tucked a napkin into her collar, picked up her spoon, and set it down again. "It's a lot for a girl your age, having to carry the family legacy on your own. I am sorry about that."

"Well, not just me. There's you, too," I reminded her.

"Course, you're right. But . . . your mama . . . oh, she was a one! I do miss her."

Though I'd never met her, I missed her, too.

"When she died," I said slowly, "weren't you even a little tempted to wish her back?"

Gram's face turned dour. "Not even once. Eat your soup."

It was rainy that night, so I put on my long coat and snuck one of our precious few candles from the closet to light my way through the trees. As I walked, I shielded the flame with one hand. Though it was only partway through autumn, the warmth on my skin felt delicious.

The leafy earth sloshed a little under my feet. I must've scared a family of foxes out of the clearing; a few shadowy cat-dog shapes darted off as I approached.

It was cloudy, so I couldn't see much in the way of stars. Would that yap things up, or would my whistle carry just the same, clear sky or no?

I blew out my candle, set it aside, and held my cup up high. In the darkness, against the backdrop of the sky, I could see my hands shaking. I had to try three times to get my lips to form a whistle. When I finally did produce a sound, it was a pitiful little crooning. A sleepy bird warbled back. I'd have to do better than that.

The coach at school had told me more than once that a bad basketball player—like myself—could get better by picturing herself, in her mind's eye, shooting perfect baskets. To be honest, hoops weren't that important to me, so I never tried it, but I thought this might be just the occasion to apply Coach Tyler's wisdom.

I closed my eyes and imagined myself making a sharp, clear whistle. I imagined the starlight pouring down into my cup, a silver liquid with the smell of carnations. I built a perfect picture in my mind until I was barely one percent shy of believing I'd already done it—and then I whistled into the night for real.

You wouldn't believe the sound that came out of me! Even a champion pig caller would have tipped his hat to me that night.

Time stretched like gum, and it seemed like a long wait before anything happened. Looking back, maybe only seconds passed. All at once, a patch of clouds appeared to thin some and turn a little brighter, thinner and brighter, thinner and brighter, until a hole appeared, and in that space I could see the clear sky and a single star shimmering a little red, a little blue.

It was bigger than any star should be, and I knew it was

my star, the star I'd been born under, the star that watched over me, and would until I took my very last breath. But you know what else? It was more than a star, too. It was the face of someone who cared about me more than anyone else ever could or had. A face, even though I can't say I saw eyes or nose or anything like that. Right then, I found myself thinking of what Gram had said about wish fetchers being the underlings of angels.

I would have started feeling silly for thinking that sort of tootle, but there it came! Silver light started pouring from the sky. It was just as I'd seen it in my head, but a thousand times brighter. It was a silver like no one had ever imagined before, as pure as a baby's first breath, and as sweet. By the time the first drop hit the bottom of my cup, the smell of carnations was so strong my eyes began to tear up, but in a nice way.

When I'd caught the last of the starlight, the hole in the clouds closed over, and you never would have thought a scrap of light could have pierced that blanket-covered sky. I lowered the cup gingerly so as not to spill the precious stuff.

Now what? I wondered.

I realized with a jolt that I didn't have any pockets, so I didn't have any lint! How would I make a wish seed, the way Gram had done? After two full minutes of worry, I remembered what Gram had said about me finding my own way, and about how her ma used to drink the starlight, while

Gram poured it as if she was watering a plant. What would my way be? What should it be?

I looked at that cup and thought of all the things a person could do with something that pours. You could fill a pot and boil something in it. You could put it in a bottle and spray it. You might even wash your feet in it. I wondered and pondered, and kept coming back to the idea of cooking something with it. (I don't believe that will come as much of a surprise to you, since food had been on my mind a lot those last few months.) All right, then, some type of *wish snack*, but what?

Just then I remembered that big bag of flour sitting in our kitchen. Gram hadn't used but a smidge of it making those dumplings, so there was plenty left.

What if . . . ?

What if I mixed up the starlight with flour and made biscuits?

Wish biscuits!

Careful, so careful, I carried my cup home and managed not to spill a drop. When I got there, Pa was away and Gram's light still shone beneath her door, so I didn't have to trouble myself too much with being quiet. I took out the flour, a big bowl, and a baking sheet. We didn't have much lard left, so I let that be, hoping the sort of magic one would find in pure starlight would keep it from sticking to the pan too badly.

I poured and stirred until I had a mixture that looked something like the glitter paste my art teacher made. With a big spoon, I heaped four dollops of dough onto the baking sheet.

There was one little hitch, and I didn't realize it until I was sliding the biscuits into the oven: ovens run on electricity, and electricity costs money. It was one thing to fetch wishes for the good of others, but it was another to fetch wishes to your own detriment. I was already using some of our precious flour. Should I run up an electric bill that we couldn't pay, too?

But, you know, sometimes the little voice inside you whispers, and even though it may not make a lot of sense at first, it hits you all of the sudden—*There might be something to that!* Just such an idea came to me then.

I took my finger and ran it along the inside of the cup, catching the dregs of the starlight. Then I touched my finger to the oven's heating element. It turned red and hot so fast I hardly had time to pull my hand away! Quickly, I slid the pan in and shut the door.

About fifteen minutes later, the smell of wish biscuits lured Gram from her room.

"What are you cooking at this hour?" she asked.

I beamed. "Wish biscuits."

She raised an eyebrow. "I never would have thought of that." I think she was impressed.

"Hope it's all right, I used some of the flour." I nodded toward the bag.

Gram looked at the flour and cocked her head. "This flour? Dilly's flour?"

"That all right?"

"Fine, honey, except that there's not one handful less than there was after lunch." She gave the bag a squeeze. "It was this bag you used?"

I nodded. "What other flour do we have?"

She conceded my point with a bob of her head. "Well, ain't that something. Miracle flour. Seventy-nine years in this town and Sass still has the power to surprise me."

Gram hovered over me as I eased the biscuits from the oven. They were as perfect as any bread you ever saw. Golden brown on top, fluffy white down below, and perfectly round.

"Bee-u-ti-ful!" Gram gushed.

It would have been one of life's perfect moments, had my stomach not grumbled right then.

"Why are you frowning?" Gram set a hand on my shoulder. "We've got miracle flour! I don't know about you, but I'm having fry bread."

Seeing as how Gram and I were up late snacking on fry bread, I didn't get as much sleep as I might have. I was late rising and late leaving, so I had to rush to the library to meet Jura, like we'd planned.

JoBeth Haines, town librarian and police dispatcher, smiled as I walked in.

"Genuine! Good thing you stopped by! The new *Georgia History Today* just came in." She slid the magazine over the counter, along with the *Sass Settee,* our biweekly newspaper. "My column's in the *Settee,* you know. 'Police Beat.' Page three."

"Thanks, Missus Haines. I can't wait to read it."

I gave the *Settee*'s headlines a quick glance: PACK YOUR UMBRELLA, SAYS WEATHER BUREAU! and SASS-Y CHILI RECIPE FEATURED ON COOKING CHANNEL!

I looked around the library. It didn't take long, seeing as how the place was half the size of my schoolroom. Still, it was stacked floor-to-ceiling with books, giving it a cozy sort of feel.

Both computer stations were empty.

"Missus Haines, did you see a girl in here today? A stranger, about my age?" I asked.

JoBeth was about to reply when the police radio squawked. She held up a finger and mouthed, *Hang on.* Deputy Lamar asked her to check some license plate numbers, which she did before turning her attention back to me.

"There was a young lady in here earlier," she said. "Saw her yesterday, too. She fiddled with the computer for a while, then asked where she could get a mocha latte. I'm pretty sure that's fancy coffee, so I sent her over to Ham's."

I stuffed my reading material into my satchel and darted across the street to the diner.

A bell jangled overhead as I entered. Scree Hopkins sat with her tenth-grade boyfriend on the pill-shaped stools at the counter. She gave me a Hey-Genuine-look-at-me-with-my-tenth-grade-boyfriend! kind of look, which I answered with my own That's-great-I'll-see-you-in-homeroom-like-everybody-else-anyway smile. Aside from them two, and someone in one of the booths, the place was empty.

"Genuine Sweet!" Ham, a pink-cheeked feller with a crewcut, slapped the counter. "I see you came for one of my fine apple fritters!"

Don't tell no one, but I sometimes thought of Ham as my almost-pa. He looked out for me. Plus, he'd known my ma real well. Whenever he found me feeling chewed up or sad, he'd sit me down and tell me some peart tale about the good woman Cristabel Sweet had been.

"That does sound tasty, Ham. Maybe some other time," I said. Of course, what I truly meant was, "Aw, Ham, you know I'm so poor I can't even pay attention," but a girl's got to have some pride.

The person in the booth turned to look my way. It was Jura. A frothy coffee sat before her.

"I'll just join my friend over there, if that's all right," I told Ham.

"Sittin's free," he replied, swatting my shoulder with his dishrag.

I walked to the booth and slid in across from Jura.

"Hi, Genuine." She practically shone in her fine city clothes.

"I'm late for school, so I can't stay, but I brought you something," I said, reaching into my bag.

"What is it?" Jura leaned forward in her seat, trying to sneak a peek.

"It's a wish biscuit." I offered Jura the biscuit bundled in a handkerchief. Before I left home that morning, I'd whispered to it that Jura's ma needed a job in Sass. "Don't let the waitress see. She might not appreciate us bringin' non-tippable food in here."

Jura opened the cloth. Her eyes grew wide. "Ohh!" She drew a long breath over the biscuit. "Just the smell of it! I love homemade! My granny used to make these!"

"Shh!" I hushed her, dipping my head toward the counter. "Your granny's weren't quite like this one, I reckon. Now, promise you'll eat the whole thing, all right?"

"I wouldn't waste a crumb! Thanks, Genuine." She pulled a piece off and popped it in her mouth before tucking it into her bag.

Scree screeched a giggle. I spun around in a panic, thinking I'd been overheard, but she was only laughing at something her beau had said. Maybe I was getting jumpy after Gram's talk about not stirring folks up with my wish fetching.

"That biscuit is *really* good," Jura told me. "You should *sell* those or something."

Then she reached across the table and grasped my hand. "Thanks for doing this for me and my mom. It means a lot."

I swallowed hard. She truly meant it. I may not have known Jura well, but even I could see this wish would take a real load off her shoulders. When you can help folks in a way that fills them with such sincere appreciation, why would you want to keep that secret?

"Ain't nothin' but a thing." I waved a hand like I was clearing the air. "But you've got to know I haven't even conjured so much as a sunrise at dawn yet."

"But you will," she insisted. "You're going to be really good at this. I know it."

Go figure. There was somebody right in my very own Sass, Georgia, who *believed* in me. Besides Gram, I mean.

"Well, if you're gonna live here, you'll be needing this." I reached into my satchel and pulled out the newspaper. "Can't call yourself Sassy unless you read the *Settee*."

"Better news than nothing." She laughed. "I can't take any more Channel Two *Fo Sho Cajun Cooking*!"

"Don't you talk trash about Boudreaux Thibodeaux in *my* town, *cher*," I teased.

"Gen'wine, you a wish fetcher fo' sho'!" Jura spun the worst Cajun accent I'd ever heard. "Go take care of your bizness, *cher*, den let's get on with saving the world, aw-rite?"

I couldn't help laughing, but I confess, a part of me sat back real still and serious, thinking things over. Sure, I could keep my wish fetching quiet. Because it was true: you never did know how some folks might respond. But keeping quiet might also keep me hungry in a world that didn't see fit to feed a person just because she had a mouth. Whether a body dies at the hands of the mob with pitchforks or dies of starvation and lack of heat—they both amount to the same thing. The end of all breathing.

I'd have to wait and see if Jura's wish biscuit came to anything. But if it did, well, maybe my new friend was right. Maybe it was time to stir the pot.

4

SUPPLY AND DEMAND

I N MY GRADE, THE SEVENTH GRADE, THERE WERE SIX kids, including me. There were four in eighth, five in the ninth, and a whopping nine people in tenth. The eleventh and twelfth grades were so small—three people put together—that they met in the same room. The younger ones—we called 'em ankle biters—all had classes in our school, too, a big-ish building made of the same red brick they used to build the city hall/police department/library.

It won't take long to familiarize you with my classmates, so I'll do that now. There was Danny (who went by Chester), Sligh (who went by Donut), Martin (who glared at you no matter what you called him), and Sonny Wentz (who I always thought was kind of cute). Me and Scree Hopkins (who I told you about) were the only girls at that point, and she didn't have much time for me, seeing as how she and Micky Forks were attached at the lips.

Our teacher is Mister Strickland, and he does have a reputation for strick-ness, if you take my meaning, but I still like him because he's careful about answering people's questions until they really understand the answers.

He wasn't too happy with me that particular morning, though.

"Genuine Sweet, where is your mind?" By his tone of voice, I reckoned he'd asked me something and I'd replied by staring out the window.

Actually, my mind was on wish biscuits and how they might be turned to the sort of profit that would pay an electric bill. What if I *did* have the MacIntyre shine and Jura's wish really came true? Could I charge money for fetching? What *was* a reasonable cost for a wish?

"Sorry, sir," I said.

"'Sorry, sir,' is not an answer," he pressed.

"I guess I was thinking about . . . economics, sir. Scarcity and demand. That sort of thing." As I may have mentioned, I don't like to lie.

He gave me a long look. "That would be downright respectable if we weren't in the middle of reading *Macbeth*. I want two pages on my desk tomorrow, on the economics of *paying* proper attention in class, yes?"

"Yes, sir," I agreed with obligatory sullenness.

Secretly, I kind of liked writing essays for Mister Strickland. He let me think big thoughts on paper, and he underlined important ideas, making comments like, "Follow this rabbit down the warren and you'll really have something." I figured I might write this essay about the costs and benefits of devoting oneself to an education. For instance, *Cost: Valuable cooking-channel-watching time is lost. Benefit: An education might well prepare one to be a chef with a show on the cooking channel.*

Concerning the question of electric bills and wishes, I postponed my deliberations until lunch, seeing as how Mister Strickland would have a wide eyeball turned my way for the rest of the morning.

Lunch was consternating for two reasons. First, the food was awful—but it was filling. To eat or not to eat? Given my circumstances, I believe you know the answer to *that* question. The other problem was a little hairier. See, there was this boy, Travis Tromp, same age as me but in a lower grade because he got held back.

Travis fabled himself as a sort of rebel, but he wasn't a very successful one. Far as I could tell, he was mostly just angry. About hunters *and* animal rights-ers, overgrown yards *and* code enforcers. Goodness forbid somebody expressed an opinion in front of him—he always took the other side. Loudly. And never by invitation. I think he tried to make himself unpleasant to be around. There were only two things in the world he liked: basil cigarettes and me. If the smell was any indication, basil cigarettes were as revolting as they sounded, but his ma was a seller of herbs and such, so I guess the stuff was lying around. Regarding the other, well, let's just say I had my strategies.

On this particular day, I waited outside the cafeteria door until Travis—wearing all black, as usual—sat down and started to eat. Then I found a seat that was blocked on both sides—by Donut on the right and Sonny on the left. (Sitting next to Sonny did give me warm shivers, but you won't repeat that, will you?) Engirdled in that way, I opened my milk, opened my notebook, and wrote:

Number of wishes I might fetch each week = ?
Amount of money I need to bring in weekly = ??
?? divided by ? = cost per wish

If only I knew for sure that I *could* fetch a wish! Hopefully, it wouldn't take long for Jura's biscuit to go to work. Missus Fuller's gas had appeared overnight, after all.

"Move," said an all-too-familiar voice.

"Eat a turd, Travis," Sonny replied. I fancied this was him sticking up for his right to sit by me. Warm shiver number two.

"Don't make me tell you, Donut." Travis poked Donut in the shoulder.

I don't expect it would have really come to blows. Travis

was actually kind of skinny, and I thought he kept his dark hair long mostly so he could hide behind it. But Donut sighed, gave me a look of mild apology, and went off to sit with Mister Strickland.

"Hey, baby."

And there I was, back with my lunch buddy, Mister Blackshirt Blackpants Blackington.

"If you respected me at all, Travis, you'd call me by my name," I told him.

"Shore I respect you, *Genuine*. But a man thinks of his girl as 'baby.' It's a habit."

I didn't even acknowledge the "his girl" comment. "Like those noxious things you're always smoking?"

"I'd quit in a flash, if you asked me to."

I wasn't going to be roped in. "I'm kind of busy right now, Travis."

Sonny broke in. "How's life in the third grade, Travis?"

"Sixth. *Sixth* grade," Mister Blackpants corrected. "Busy with what, sugar?"

I rolled my eyes.

Sonny sighed, loudly setting down his fork. "Mister Strickland asked me to clean the blackboards for him. If you're not too busy, I could use a hand." This invitation was wonderfully, blessedly directed at me.

Busy? Who said I was busy? "Sure, Sonny."

Travis disappeared completely from my mind, as did the

cafeteria and all the people in it. Sonny and I scraped out our trays, dropped them in the bin, and I floated out the door after him.

Later, Scree Hopkins deigned to tell me that Travis looked real vexed as Sonny and I sauntered off together.

Here's what I'd like to say about what happened in that empty classroom, me and Sonny alone: *None of your business.*

Here's what really happened: a lot of blackboard washing and the exchange of two incomplete sentences.

"Thanks for, uh . . ." I mumbled.

"Welcome," Sonny mumbled back.

Still, I treasured the memory of those words until the last bell rang.

After that, though, my thoughts drifted back to biscuits and wishing. Once food and heat were taken care of, how *would* it be to step out some? I confess I took some pleasure in daydreaming that I, Genuine Sweet, might mend some great catastroke with the mere flick of a wish. Wouldn't it be a marvel to hear someone say, *That Genuine sure did save the day with that wish fetching of hers! Dangerous Dale Sweet's daughter made good after all!* And maybe Sonny would be there, and might reply, *I don't know what this town would do without her!*

★ ★ ★

"Genuine! You won't believe this! Look!" A friendly hand shook the latest *Sass Settee* under my nose.

Jura found me standing outside Sass Foods, contemplating whether I had enough lost-and-found change to buy a chicken breast for Gram to fix with supper.

"Jura! Hey!" I stuffed the money into my pocket. "I haven't seen you for a couple days! How's things?"

"Look!" she repeated, all jiggles and grins.

I took the paper from her. She'd circled an ad with a waxy black line. It read, *Help Wanted, Auto Mechanic, must have experience with foreign cars.*

"All . . . right," I said, waiting for Jura to explain.

"That's my mom! That's what my mom does! She fixes cars!" Jura fairly trembled with excitement. "I decided you were right. If I'm going to stay in Sass, I have to stay informed. So, when the new *Settee* came out today, I picked one up. And there it was!" She poked the page so hard I thought she'd put her finger through it.

"I called my mom and told her about the ad and she called the garage and they had this whole huge talk on the phone and—" She paused to gasp for breath. "I just know they want to hire her! I can feel it in my bones!"

I couldn't help noticing the double thump of my own heartbeat as I watched a real wish—a wish that I had fetched—get fulfilled right before my eyes.

"Does she, uh, know much about foreign cars?" I asked a little nervously.

Jura nodded wildly. "Japanese cars. German cars. She even has a Fisk Certificate!"

"What's that?"

"It says she can repair these new cars from Norway. They don't even hit the market until January. They're gonna be *huge*. And my mom's only one of a hundred people in the whole country that knows how to fix them. Bet you people from all over will be coming to Sass, Georgia, to get their Fisks fixed!"

By now, I was hoppingly excited myself. "And you won't have to go back to your old school!" I exclaimed.

She rolled her eyes with the bliss of it. "I *know!* I'm really free! Plus, my aunt Trish—I've never seen her so happy!" Jura said. "Oh, Genuine, it's so crazy. I didn't even dare to hope for it. I mean, look at this paper. There's two job openings in all of Sass—the mechanic one and a security job at the retirement home. What are the chances, you know?"

"I'm just pitched for you, Jura." And I meant it. Her happiness was contagious.

"This is a sign, Genuine. You and me, we're gonna be unstoppable! I can't wait to see what we'll do next!" Jura took my hands and pulled me into a big hug.

Let me tell you, there is nothing like the feeling you get

when you've really helped somebody. Nothing could douse my smile!

Turned out I didn't have enough for that chicken breast, but I practically danced home anyway.

Principles are all well and good, but when I got home and found Gram fretting over an overdue bill — second notice — I sank down to earth right quick.

There was no avoiding it. It was time for me to set up shop.

I took three wish biscuits and headed to Miss Faye's Hair, Nails, Beauty Supply, and Leatherworks. Faye, a relative of my pa's, was a big woman, always smiling. I liked her very much.

"Hey, cuz!" I called, swinging the door open wide.

It takes new customers a little time to get used to the mash of odors at Faye's — nail-polish remover and hide-tanning formula — but I was long used to it. I quick-glanced around to get a feel for my audience. Three local ladies sat under those helmet-style hair dryers, cackling over a little he-said, she-said. Another soaked her nails.

Faye looked up from the leather she was stitching. "Genuine! What brings you to my fine establishment?"

She was busy, so I got right down to it. "I'm sort of

starting a business, and I thought you might let me make an announcement to your customers."

"Shore! What sort of business?"

"Wish fetching," I replied.

"What's that?"

"You know, granting people's wishes," I explained.

Her smile fell a little as she tried to puzzle this out. "You mean, like doing their chores when they's too busy?"

"No. Like, 'I wish I may, I wish I might.' Ping! Wish granted."

Faye nodded slowly. "That's an interesting line of work you've chosen."

I would not be deterred. "So, can I? Make my announcement?"

"Be my guest! They sure ain't goin' nowhere!" she told me, smiling again. "You sure you wouldn't rather sell hand-wove potholders, though?"

Figuring some things only suffer by explanation, I left to fetch a box from the supply room. Setting it in the center of the salon, I gave Faye a nod.

"Y'all listen up!" Faye called from the nail station, where she was now trimming Missus Binset's cuticles. "Genuine's got something to say!"

The ladies' jawing died down. Three pink-rollered heads turned my way.

I hopped up on my box. "Thank you for your, uh, allowing me to interrupt your, uh, fancifying regimens."

"Probably taking up a collection for her daddy's bail," I heard one of them whisper.

I felt my cheeks turn red.

"Go ahead, sugar." Faye gave me an encouraging bob of the head.

"Um," I began. "So—I'm Genuine. Guess y'all know that. And, uh, I'm here to ask y'all to think on something in your lives that isn't quite as fine as you'd like it to be. Maybe you've got more chores than you can manage. Or your bunions might be troubling you, and nothing but nothing will give you relief. Every one of us has things we need, you see. And that's where I hope to be of, uh, service."

I paused to give each lady some eye-to-eye contact.

"Not long ago, a woman needed work in Sass. *Sass!* you might say. *There ain't no work in Sass!* And, of course, you'd be right. But I was able to help her out, and in less than three days' time, she had her a job in town! *How?* you might ask."

No one did ask, which deflated me some, but I went on. "By sending her to the day labor office? No, ma'am! I used my own special inheritance! I'm a fourth-generation wish fetcher, you see. And I believe *I* might be able to fetch *you* the special things your hearts are longing for! Now, uh—"

Here came the hard part. Could I really ask these women

to pay me cash money for wishes? And if I did, could I really fetch the kinds of things they'd ask for? What if Jura's ma's job was a fluke? What if Dangerous Dale's daughter turned out to be nothing more than a well-meaning yap-up? I almost stepped shamefacedly down off my box right then. But, all at once, I recalled Gram's troubled expression as she studied that overdue bill. *No!* I determined. I would *not* go all feather-legged now!

I swallowed hard and went on. "For the reasonable price of twenty dollars, I'll give you one of these here biscuits." I held one up for display. "And through the power of my family shine, you will—almost certainly—very probably—I'm thinking the chances are real good that your wish will come true. And if it doesn't, I swear I'll refund your money! Give it a couple weeks first, though. Maybe a month, to be on the safe side. Um. Actually, I'm not sure how long a wish would take, if it was a hard one—"

I saw that I'd drifted downriver some, so I grabbed a paddle and rowed myself back. "Well. That's all. Twenty dollars a wish, satisfaction guaranteed. Thank you kindly for your time." I plastered on the biggest grin I could muster, curtsied, and hopped off the box.

"I tell you what I'd wish for!" Missus Hoover said at once. "That Reggie Booker would close his blame window blinds at night! Him and his new lady friend been working all kinds of hoodoo over there!"

"Hmmph," grumped Penny Walton, turning her magazine pages with an angry flick. For some reason I couldn't discern, she glared at me every now and again.

"Twenty dollars is a cheap price for a wish come true," Faye said sagely. My cousin may not have understood the wish-fetching trade, but that didn't stop her from trying to drum up a little business for me. Still, she did look a mite worried as she whispered in my direction, "You really can magic stuff up with those biscuits?"

"Yes, ma'am. I believe I can," I replied.

Penny Walton pulled the hair dryer from her own head and stormed over.

"Who do you people think you are?" she snarled.

I looked over my shoulder for all those "people" she was referring to. No one was there. "Ma'am?"

"MacIntyres! Wish fetchers!" she caterwauled. Turning to Missuses Hoover and Kalweit, under the dryers, she added, "Don't let her draw you into her schemes, girls! Her kind won't bring anything but trouble!"

Faye stepped away from her work, poised to defend me, should things take a turn.

Penny Walton directed her dagger-eye my way. "You think I don't recall the hopes Cristabel dredged up, then cast away? Think again!" She set a hand on her hip and poked a finger in my face. "You drop this flummery now, or *I'll* put a stop to it!"

She marched out the door before Faye could finish shouting about the rollers still in Penny's hair.

I sat for a time, not sure what to make of any of it.

Libby Kalweit, sitting under her hair dryer, said to Faye, "Switch this off, would you, honey?"

Once the dryer was off, Libby told me, "Don't let Penny hurt your feelings none. If anyone should be ashamed, it's the pot-stirrers who turned a sorrow into a spectacle."

"What *are* you talking about, Libby?" Faye asked before I could.

Missus Kalweit glanced my way. "I don't want to say too much. Make me just as bad as the muckrakers."

When we kept silent, waiting for more, she went on, "All right. Without saying too much, poor Penny's heart got broke. Bad. Still, the pain might have passed in time, were it not for her so-called friends poking at the sore places. Spreading lies, getting Penny all stirred up. Nobody believed the things those girls said about your mama, of course, but poor Cristabel still went home every day for a month, cryin'."

"Hush now, Libby!" Missus Binset hissed. "There's no call to go dredging up the past!"

"You hush! You're just feelin' guilty for how you and Penny fabled against poor Cristabel! Trying to rile folks up so they'd turn their backs on her!" Missus Kalweit said tartly. "Far as I'm concerned, there's no fault in the MacIntyre line. Not a one of you!" she assured me. A few seconds later, she muttered, "Though your granny never charged money for her wishes."

My gut twisted with a flash of anger. I wanted to say, *What should I do, old woman, feed you with wishes while I starve?* It took everything I had to remember that, thanks to Dilly Barker's flour, I hadn't had a single hunger pain in two days.

"Times change," was all I said.

"That may be, but I don't know many folks with twenty dollars to spare," said Libby.

Faye waved a hand, calling me to her. "I'm sure it's not your fault, Genuine, Penny gettin' so worked up," she said. "She works in real estate, and the market's bad, you know? When people get stressed, they take things out on folks who don't deserve it. That's probably what it was."

Whatever it was, when Faye closed up shop, I still had three biscuits and my wallet was empty. I was gonna have to come at this differently.

5

A FINE NOTION

WHEN TRAVIS TROMP TRIED TO LATCH ON TO me in the hall the next morning, I went right up to Sonny and asked if he needed help washing blackboards again.

"You seem a little chewed up today, Genuine," Sonny said as he pulled a piece of fruit from his locker.

"A little." I was, after all, a wish fetcher with nary a wish to fetch.

He held up his orange. "Want half?"

"I'd love it!" I said, maybe a little more dramatically than the moment called for. But I really did love it—the orange and the fact that Sonny was sharing it with me, of his own free will.

Later, Scree gripped my sleeve and dished, "Oooh, the look on Travis's face while you ate that orange! Dear goodness!"

Maybe, I thought, *just maybe* Travis needed a wish biscuit to help him find a girl who'd love him back. Then he'd be less angry and wouldn't pester folk so much. I decided it was a good idea, and I told myself to remember: *Biscuit for Travis.* But you know how it is when life gets lively. Sometimes things slip your mind. Because, that day came a treat that brightened my spirits right up. While Mister Strickland was calling roll, Missus Forks, the school secretary, led a new student into the room.

"Class, I'd like you to meet Jura Carver," Missus Forks said. "Go on, Jura. There's a desk right next to Genuine, over there."

I waved a hand. She saw me and let out a huge breath. Her shoulders—which she'd been holding so high they might have been earrings—relaxed.

"I am so glad to see you!" she whispered to me.

"Are you all right?" I whispered back, wondering where Jura's mettle had gone.

"Ladies, let's don't make me separate you on Jura's first day, hmm?" Mister Strickland frowned at us, but I could tell it was just his way of making Jura welcome. "Genuine, will you get Miss Carver a set of books?"

I ran to the back of the room and selected the most decently clean math, history, English, and earth science books on the shelf. Even though we were almost done with

Shakespeare, I grabbed a *Macbeth,* too, so Jura could follow the last of the discussion.

"Um," she said as she examined the math book.

"Yes, Jura?" our teacher inquired.

"I'm in algebra," she replied.

Mister Strickland paused. "Are you?" After a moment, he brightened. "Well, good for you. We'll see what we can do about that. You won't mind a little review today, though, will you?"

"No, sir," she answered.

And then she didn't say another word until lunch.

I showed Jura to the lunchroom and motioned for her to go on in first. She looked right and left like she expected a truck to hit her. Figuring she was only a bit addled in new surroundings, I started to take the lead, but she set an arm in front of me, so I couldn't pass.

"Jura, what's —"

"Do you think —" Jura whispered, casting her gaze over our classmates. "I mean, these kids, you've known them for a while?"

"Since I was knee-high to a grasshopper," I told her.

"And they're . . . pretty nice?"

"Mostly," I replied. "You don't want to knock Martin's eraser off his desk the day after his pa busts him for skipping school. And Scree's been known to talk from both sides of her mouth. But there's no harm in 'em." I considered Jura's worried expression. "You've been looking awfully wary today. What's got you so creepified?"

"Waiting for the other shoe to drop, I guess." She twisted the strap of her satchel. "I know this isn't my old school, but I still half-expect somebody to sneak up on me and stick something sharp in my back."

"Like a knife?" I asked, alarmed.

"Usually it was a comb or something, but they'd let me think it was a knife. They tormented me pretty bad."

People tormented smart, sweet Jura? "That's wretched! No! There ain't a person at this table would do such a thing! I promise!"

She unclenched a little. After we collected our very sloppy joes from the lunch line, I led her to the seventh-grade table, and we sat.

"Where you live, Jura?" asked Donut, his mouth full of food.

Everyone swiveled Jura's way. In Sass, people tended to turn their neighbors into landmarks. If you were looking for Cribbs Bee Farm, "Down by the Sweet place" was no less correct than "Beside the bridge over Squirrel Tail Creek." (Of course, I knew full well that anytime someone gave directions that included "Down by the Sweet place," they also served up an earful about ol' Dangerous Dale.)

"I'm not sure exactly. Off of . . . um . . . Briggs Road? Biggs Road?" Jura waffled.

"She's Trish Spencer's kin," I filled in. "Her ma works at Dandy Andy's."

"Oh!" the whole seventh grade replied at once, satisfied.

Turning to Jura, I whispered, "She did get the job, right?"

Jura nodded back.

And that was it for Jura's welcome into our circle. She might always be a newcomer in Sass, but she'd never be a stranger again.

"You're too pretty, Jura," said Scree, who graced us with her lunchtime presence because Micky was out sick that day. "You should be a model."

This was high praise from Scree, who was herself a pageant fiend. I should say, I don't mean that disparagingly; she really was nutty about it.

"What's wrong with you, Sonny? You sick?" I heard Martin ask.

I looked at Sonny with all the womanly concern I could muster. His cheeks flared red, almost as if he was blushing.

"Do you have a fever?" I asked.

"Naw. M'fine." He turned away and waved a hand like he was swatting a fly.

Just then, Travis tromped up. It was hard to tell, but I

thought his hair might've been combed some. "I notice you're done with your tray, Genuine. Can I hump it to the trash for you?"

Scree burst out in peals of giggles. "*Hump* it?"

"I mean, what I meant was—" Travis floundered.

"No, Travis," I cut in. "I've got it."

"You can take mine," Jura said, real out of the blue. "If you want." I could tell she felt sorry for him, but of course, that was only because she didn't know him yet.

Travis gave Jura a confused look.

"Travis Tromp," I said, "this is Jura Carver, Trish Spencer's kin."

"Pleasure," Travis said, taking her tray. "Any friend of Genuine's is a genuine friend of mine."

I rolled my eyes, but Travis was already gone.

"You don't have to be nice to him on my account," I told Jura.

She shrugged. "He seems like the kind of guy who doesn't have many friends."

"That's a fact," I agreed.

"Do people tease him and stuff?" she asked.

I'd never really thought on it before. "Sometimes," I said, and realized it was true. Before Travis had had to repeat the fourth grade, he'd been in a class with me and Donut and the rest. None of us had bothered him, but the older kids gave him a hard time. Once, Travis had written a poem and Doug

Talley read it out loud in the middle of the courtyard—right before he shoved it and the rest of Travis's papers in the slimy cafeteria trash can.

Jura sighed, a whiff of anger on her breath. "Me and Travis have a lot in common."

"You do not!" I insisted.

"Enough that I had to come here." She looked away. "At Ardenville Central Middle, 'Teasing Jura Carver' was pretty much an extracurricular sport."

"Gosh. I'm sorry." It was the best I could come up with. What do you say to a thing like that? "I'm glad you're here now."

Jura brushed a few crumbs off the table. Then she seemed to make a decision. She sat up straighter and threw her shoulders back.

"Me, too." She held out her fist.

I looked at it for a second or two. "What?"

"Bump it!" She laughed. "You don't do this here?"

I tapped her fist with my fist. "What's it mean?"

"It means, you and me, we're tight," Jura replied.

"Huh. I've never been tight before," I confided. "What do we do now?"

She thought it over. "How about I help you save the world?"

"Ye-ah, I've gotta figure out how to feed myself first." I

told her about my sad attempt to raise a little cash at Faye's. "Folks just don't have the dollars to spare."

"Hmm." For a time, Jura vanished down some dusty trail in her mind. "If money's the problem . . ." She bit her lip. "People do grow their own food around here, right? Why couldn't you offer to trade wishes with farmers — for vegetables and meat and stuff? You know, like bartering?"

It didn't take me half a blink to see the wisdom in that. "I might even be able to trade for house repairs!"

"And who knows?" Jura added, getting excited now. "Maybe the president of the electric company has a dream only a wish fetcher can fulfill!"

"Bartering!" I marveled. Heck, even my ma had done it, trading wishes for the promise of good deeds paid forward. "You got a head *full* of sense, girl!"

"And *then* we can save the world." She smiled.

I raised my eyebrows. "You really think we could?"

"Yeah, I do."

"All right, but I'm not sure how to go about it," I said.

"I'll research it. You just focus on your bartering."

In the time it took me to walk home, a mantle of gray clouds set in. I found Gram pacing the front porch, wringing her hands. My heart sank. Had she heard about the dustup at the salon? Was she upset? I waited for the verdict.

But all she said when I walked up was, "Hungry?"

I said I was.

Gram insisted she didn't need help with dinner, so while she worked, I went ahead and told her everything that had gone on at Faye's, particularly Penny Walton's wish-hampering fit.

"I don't know why she had to take it so personal!" I was fairly riled, now that I thought on it.

Gram smiled weakly as she turned the opener on our canned hash.

"She's got a bee in her bonnet, is all," she finally spoke. "It's nothing against you, precisely."

"Sure seemed like it was!" I started chopping one of the last carrots from this year's pitiful garden.

"Folks just don't like to be poked." She took the knife from me and started in on the carrots. "Maybe you ought not to do something like that again."

"Poked?" I gaped. "Gram! I didn't go there to poke anyone! I was trying to scrounge up some money for bills!"

Gram dropped her head. "Sit down for a minute, Gen. I want to say something to you."

I huffed, but I sat.

She joined me at the table and set her hand on my hand. "Worry never filled a belly."

"But—"

"Birds don't sit awake at night wondering if they'll find

seeds in the morning—and yet good folks keep filling bird feeders, don't they?" Gram asked.

"Yes, but—"

"Can you break a drought by pacing the floor and thinking on how dry you feel? Can you force a flower to bloom by pulling a bud apart?"

"No, but—"

"No. You'd only ruin the flower." Gram held up a finger before I could object again. "Listen. I'm not saying you do nothing while you waste away of starvation. Living in this world takes action. What I am saying is, *consider what actions you take.*"

"But even *you* said you were worried about practical things!"

Gram started to say something more, but her hand fluttered to her mouth and she fell quiet.

After a time, she took up her spoon. "Just promise me you'll be more careful, all right?"

That night, the storm clouds burst, tapping out a tinny rhythm of raindrops on our roof. As I burrowed into the cushions of our tired old sofa, I considered my actions. What I'd done and what I might do yet. And I considered some other things, too. Like, how the starlight that twinkled through the living room window shone from the very same stars that had once shone down on Gram in her girlhood, and even on my wish-fetching great-gram. My ma had also wished on those stars, shining her own special light on the strangers of Ardenville.

On the other hand, they were the same stars whose wishing power had destroyed the once-great city of Fenn.

Maybe Penny Walton's friends had heard that story, too.

Our house mouse, Scooter, darted across the floor. I sighed. Repairs on the house. Food. Heat. We needed those things. Desperately. And with no job in sight for Pa—nor even a whiff of hope that he was trying to find one—I was coming to believe I was the only one who could save us.

"Sorry, Gram," I whispered, flinging my blanket aside. "You'll just have to trust me to make things right."

I went to the kitchen table and lit a candle. Then, while Gram slept and Pa snored, I crafted three letters.

Dear Handyman Joe
or Miz Tromp
or Chickenlady Snopes,

Genuine Sweet here, and thank you kindly for reading this letter.

The reason I am writing is to inquire whether you might be interested in a trade. I am offering real wishes (good-hearted ones, not things like wishing something bad would happen to someone who wronged you) in exchange for items like food or house repairs.

I know this might seem too good to be true, but I am in fact a real wish fetcher, descended from a line of wish fetchers. I am only just learning to use my shine, but I promise it's real and I'll do my very best to fetch the thing you wish for.

To sweeten the pot, I'll allow you to pay me ONLY AFTER you've seen with your own eyes that I've truly fetched your wish.

If you are interested, you can visit me at Ham's Diner this afternoon, 3:30 to 6:30 p.m.

Most sincerely,

Genuine Sweet

On the way to school the next morning, I put each of the letters in their respective mailboxes.

That's when things really started cooking.

6

INVITATION

FTER SCHOOL, I RACED TO HAM'S DINER TO SEE IF
my wish-trade letters had gleaned any interest.

The bell jangled as I swung the door open.

Ham greeted me from the kitchen. "Well, if it ain't Sass's
very own wish fetcher!"

I wasn't real surprised. In a place like Sass, word does get
around. The diner's two patrons turned in their seats to give
me a gander.

A few seconds later, Ham emerged from the back with a
plate of fresh apple fritters.

"Hey, Ham," I said with a little wave.

"One of these has your name on it." He held out the fritters, wafting some of those tasty fumes my way.

Oh, but they smelled good! "Not today, thanks. Actually,
I was wondering if you'd mind if I borrowed one of your
booths."

"Take your pick." He waved a hand at the empty tables.

No sooner had I sat than an apple fritter appeared on a plate in front of me.

"On the house," said Ham.

"Thank you!" A little hesitantly, I added, "I wonder . . . would you mind if I wrapped half to take home for Gram?"

He smiled kindly. "I'll get you a little bag."

I looked out the window to see if any of my invitees were on their way. Not yet, but I did glimpse Penny Walton walking down the street, stopping off at one shop, then another, leaving stacks of real estate brochures.

At 3:45, the door chime jangled and Miz Tromp came walking in. I sat up taller in my seat so she could see me. She came right over.

Miz Tromp looked a lot like Travis, with all the same dark hair and eyes and everything, but she wore regular colors like a normal person, so it was easy to forget she had such a peculiar son.

"I received your note," she said to me.

"I thought that might be why you come," I replied happily. "Wanna sit?"

She set her purse on the table and joined me. "I was excited to get your letter, Genuine." Leaning in, she lowered her voice to a whisper. "See, I have a really big wish. I don't suppose you can do really big wishes?"

I wanted to be forthright, but I was also fairly desperate

to make the trade, so I said, "Big or little, a wish is a wish, I'd think. But of course, if for some reason I can't do the job, I wouldn't expect you to pay me."

She dipped her head. "Fair enough. Now. Since it's a very big wish, I'd think you'd deserve a right sizable payment. How would you feel about a bag of fresh veggies every week until the garden peters out, and then a box of canned after that?"

My eyes went wide. "For how long?"

"Let's say . . . a year."

"That's a very generous offer, ma'am. Are you sure that seems quite fair?" I asked, feeling I had to inquire, even though a big part of me said to just hush up and accept the windfall.

"It *is* a very big wish," Miz Tromp said.

"Well, all right. What is it?" I asked.

She looked over her shoulder, but of course the only thing she could see behind her was the back of the booth.

"As you might know," she said, still whispering, "Travis's father left us when Travis was seven. Truth be told, I wish he'd left sooner. That way, at least, Travis wouldn't remember him." She squinted at the harshness of her own words. "I don't mean that Kip was a *bad* guy. He was just . . . a visionary. And he thought big dreams and small towns didn't mix." She sighed. "Anyhow, Travis is pretty angry about his dad taking off—about everything, really."

"I noticed," I told her.

"It's not Travis's fault. It hurts to have your own father set you aside."

"Yeah. I reckon so." Not that I'd know much about that.

She shrugged. "And me, I'm pretty lonely. It's hard to be a mother and a woman on one's own."

"Sure. Surely. Yes," I agreed, trying to bring my thoughts back around to Miz Tromp's quandary.

"So, this is my wish," Miz Tromp went on. "I wish for a good man. A husband for me and a father for Travis. As you well know, there are but a few single men in this town—" She made a face.

I couldn't help thinking that she was thinking of my father.

"—so I've long known my chances of finding Mister Right in Sass are pretty slim. Maybe he'd be a new customer or something. I'm not sure how it would work. That part I guess I'd leave up to you." Miz Tromp paused. "Think you can do it?"

I took a deep breath. "There's only one way to find out."

Reaching into my pack, I revealed one of the wish biscuits. "A fine husband for Miz Tromp and a good father to Travis," I whispered to the baked good.

I waited a few seconds to let the magic sink in, then I slid the biscuit over to Travis's ma. She looked at it, apparently a mite confused.

"You have to eat it," I told her.

"Now?" she asked.

"The sooner the better, if you want your man."

She gave a little laugh, then took the biscuit in hand. When she bit into it, her eyes brightened. "Dog my cats, Genuine! This is muh-muh-muh!" That last word was muddled by her chewing.

"Glad you like it." I smiled. "Now, I expect things *could* start happening pretty soon, but be patient, all right? I'm still figuring out how this works. It might take some time for the stars to arrange things like traffic detours and whatnot, to get your man here."

"I've been patient this long," she conceded.

A certain tightness that I hadn't noticed in her before suddenly loosened. As she was gathering up her keys and getting ready to go, she stopped and said, "It's probably not my place to say this, but . . . boys being how they are . . ."

"Ma'am?"

"My Travis is real fond of you—"

I held up my hand. "Miz Tromp, I like you very much. Enough to be honest with you, so here it is. Travis is as rude and contrary as they come. No girl in her right mind would put up with his *baby*s and *sugar*s. And the way he treats people—!" I didn't spell it out, for kindness' sake. She understood me. "But I am sorry that his daddy's leaving hurt him so much."

Strangely, my words didn't seem to bother her at all.

"You're a smart girl, Genuine Sweet. You let me know how that wish progresses, all right?"

Just as Miz Tromp was saying her thank-yous and farewells, Handyman Joe came strolling in. Not even troubling to sit, he offered me two full days of labor on the house—plus materials—provided I could locate an old army medal of his father's.

"I don't know if it was stole or just lost, but if you could turn it up for me, I'd be real grateful," he said. "It's all I have of him."

I thought of a necklace I had that used to be my ma's, a gold chain with a charm, a star inside a star. If I ever lost it, I'd be heartbroken. Even in the worst, most empty-bellied days, I'd never once considered selling it.

I whispered to one of the wish biscuits and gave it to Joe.

"I get the medal and a biscuit, too?" he asked.

I gave him a professional sort of nod. "That's how it works, sir. You eat the biscuit, I fetch the wish."

He patted my head and set a couple dollars on the table. "Chocolate milk's on me."

I left the diner around suppertime, Gram's half-fritter in hand. I was crossing Main Street when I heard a car horn behind me and a voice calling, "Genuine Sweet!"

Chickenlady Snopes's pickup truck pulled up to the curb, a dozen chickens cackling in cages in the back.

"Evening, ma'am!" I greeted. "Howdy, chickens!"

Miz Snopes got out of the truck and wiped her brow. "I been tearing up the pea patch trying to get to you, girl."

"Is something wrong?" Had Pa gotten himself into some kind of mess?

"No, no," she replied. "I was just wondering if that wish trade was still on the table."

"Sure is," I said. "What'd you have in mind?"

There wasn't much to it, she told me. Her hen houses were old and real rundown, and she needed some new ones.

"I'll trade you eggs *only*. I don't hold with the eating of chickens." She stood up on her toes as if she expected me to challenge her.

"Course not!" I pointed at the chickens. "They're your friends!"

"Exactly." I think she was pleased, but a mite surprised, that I agreed with her.

I pulled the last biscuit from my bag, whispered over it, "New hen houses for Chickenlady Snopes," and handed it to her.

"That's it?" she asked.

"Well, you have to eat it."

"That works out real good. I ain't had no dinner yet." She was about to climb back into her truck when she added, "You got any chickens of your own, Genuine?"

I shook my head.

"You ought to. They're good company." She drove off.

Three wishes, three trades! Creation! What else might folks wish for and have to trade? I knew Gram needed someone to fix her glasses. Lately, they'd been hanging askew on her nose. And would somebody trade a job for Pa? I wasn't even sure who to ask.

There was one thing I needed to do for sure, though, and right away. I penned a letter to the energy company offering wishes in exchange for power. Then I sang down some starlight.

When I got back inside, I found Gram busy with her knitting.

"By the by," I said as I stirred wish-biscuit dough, "you might expect some vegetables and house repairs to come our way afore long."

"Really!" Smitten with excitement, Gram set down her yarn. "How'd you manage that?"

"A man for Miz Tromp and a medal for Handyman Joe," I said.

Her smile slipped a little. "Well, you certainly are creative, child. But I thought you were gonna be more careful."

"I'm being real careful!" I promised. "I was straight-up with all of them. Told 'em if I can't fetch their wishes, they don't have to pay me. And I said I was still learning, so they'd have to be patient." I dribbled more starlight into my dough. "You do think the wishes are strong enough to find Miz Tromp a man, don't you?"

"Easy peasy," Gram assured me.

"And Handyman Joe's medal?" I asked.

"He's probably already got it in hand." She flumped down on one of the dining room chairs. "Ugh. I got as much get-up-and-go as a tortoise in a snowstorm."

"Are you sick?" I asked.

"Just tired," she replied. "Well, the bright side to those wish barters is nobody has to go without anything to get what they need. Handyman Joe gives a little time and gets rid of those spare parts he's always got lying around. And Mabel Tromp's extra vegetables might have gone to waste otherwise." Gram fiddled with her glasses. "It does make you think about Travis, some. Poor boy."

"What do you mean?" I opened the stove and touched a bit of starlight to the heating element. It glowed red.

"I guess life hasn't been easy for him."

"He doesn't make himself easy to like," I retorted. "He's snarky with everyone except me, and there, he's like something stuck to my shoes: unpleasant and hard to get away from."

Gram shrugged. "I reckon he feels that way about himself, too."

Truth to tell, I didn't fully understand what she meant by that, so I moseyed on to a different topic.

"Where's Pa?" I couldn't help wondering, if I *did* manage to wish-trade a job for him, would he even bother to show up for it?

"Oh, I imagine he's off somewhere being snarky or hard to get away from," Gram replied.

I rolled my eyes. She was probably right.

Let me tell you, that next Monday, the stars *really* started showing off.

A noise woke me early that morning—a banging sound that, at first, I feared was Pa on some kind of rampage. I put on my robe and rushed outside, index finger all poised to preach, but what I found was Gram standing on the porch, hands on her hips, smiling away as she watched Handyman Joe replace some time-and-termite-eaten boards on the side of our house.

Joe looked up from his work. "Well, if it isn't Genuine Sweet, genuine wish fetcher. You know what? My daddy's medal turned up last night."

"It did?" My belly fluttered with the excitement of it. "Where?"

"My sister found it under the cushion of an old sofa I gave her some years back," he replied. "She drove all the way from Ardenville to bring it to me. Said she had the strongest sense I might like to have it. Ha! That's some knack you ladies have." He nodded my way and tilted his head respectfully in Gram's direction, too.

Also on the porch that morning was a basket of *three* dozen eggs! A note tucked inside it read:

Miss Genuine,

A detour sent me past the Beaks Chicken Ranch yesterday. There was a sign by the road: "Free hen houses — U haul 'em." Mr. Beaks is trading it all in for a hacienda in Mexico! Bless you, Genuine. Your eggs are free for as long as I have hens.

— Caroline Snopes

Gram and I had fried eggs over miracle-flour toast that morning. No breakfast ever tasted so good!

Then, at school that day, we had pizza for lunch! I don't mean the soggy, soy-cheese variety we knew so well. The real, delivery kind, all the way from Pitney! Missus Forks told us the cafeteria oven had breathed its last, so we'd be eating takeout till the replacement came in! Between delicious bites, Jura told me she was working on the perfect plan for saving the world.

"Anytime you're ready," she told me. "How are things going with the barter?"

I told her all about my barter buddies, the eggs, and the repairs on the house.

"*Yes!*" She shot a fist into the air. "Genuine, I am *so* glad! I've been lying awake nights, worrying about you being hungry and cold."

"You have?"

Jura's brow wrinkled. "You sound surprised!"

"Well, it's awful nice of you, but I guess I wonder why."

"Why worry about you? That's a silly question. Because we're friends!"

Of course, I already knew that. But hearing it from Jura's own mouth, it warmed my heart — and gave me a certain pride. Down-home Genuine Sweet and fancy city-girl Jura Carver. Friends. Wasn't that a peach?

Now that the stars were doing their thing, I reckoned I could stop worrying about wish management for a while. I decided to use my study period to ready myself for our *Macbeth* test.

While I was reading — real absorbed, you know what I mean? When everything but the story disappears? — something bumped up against my elbow. It took me a minute to come out of my book, and by the time I looked around, no one was there. But sitting on the edge of my desk was a fine piece of chocolate wrapped in gold paper, with a note on it. It said, *I think you're sweet.*

There was no signature, but it had to be from Sonny!

Who else *could* it be? I'm sure my grin was about as dopey as a smile can be, but I couldn't help it. I squirreled the candy away in my pocket.

Later on, I tried to catch Sonny's eye to thank him, but he never seemed to look my way. I figured he was feeling shy. That was all right. I had proof of his esteem right there on my person.

But that wasn't the end of my mighty right day. Gram's glasses got mended without even having to trade a wish for it! Who would have known Mister Barker used to work for the Ardenville Eyeglassery? He happened to see how off-kilter Gram's frames were and fixed her right up. When I offered him a wish as payment, he said, "Don't talk bolliwog, Genuine. It weren't nothing at all."

Sometimes life just goes your way.

That night I told Jura I was ready to get started saving the world.

7

THE INFINITE BISCUIT THEORY

J URA WAS WAITING FOR ME OUTSIDE OF SCHOOL THAT next morning.

"Did you hear it's going to rain *again?*" she asked, shaking a *Settee* at me.

"Really? Fall is usually dry," I replied, peeking at the newspaper. ANOTHER FROG STRANGLER! it said.

"Anyway, I've been thinking about how to get maximum leverage off your superpowers," she said, pulling a spiral notebook from her satchel. It was filled with a sort of strange writing, lots of swooping loops and zigzaggy curls.

"What is that?" I asked.

"Shorthand. Old-school secretaries used to use it. It's a way to write really fast." She flipped a few pages. "Okay. First thing—"

Just then, I saw Travis's face behind the glass of the door. I had a notion he was waiting for us.

I squinched my nose. "Not here," I told Jura. A glance at the credit-union clock told me we still had a few minutes before first bell. "Follow me."

I led her to a spot I'd been visiting since my ankle-biter days, a little patch of woods just behind the school. It was through a hole in the fence, down an animal trail and up a small hill, past patches of brilliant sunlight and mosquitoey chunks of shade. Finally, we reached Sass Rock, a great gray boulder where, Ham once told me, my ma used to come to gather *her* thoughts when she was in school.

We hunkered down on the cool stone.

"So, what'cha got?" I asked.

Jura took a breath. "I've come up with three broad categories of world saving. I'll tell you what they are, you pick one, and then we'll look at specific strategies. Make sense?"

"Yes, ma'am," I said.

"Category one. Historical Intervention. We pick some terrible world event and wish it happened differently."

I was enough of an amateur historian to understand that if you pulled on one of time's threads, a whole lot else could come unraveled. "Naw. Better not."

"Okay, two. Major Planetary Intervention. We choose a worldwide issue and wish it fixed anywhere we find it. Like hunger or war."

Interesting. "All right. And three?"

"Act Locally, Think Globally. We direct all the wishing at improving the quality of life in a smaller area, like Sass or Georgia, hoping that other communities see what we're doing and do it too."

I picked up a twig and poked at a hole in my shoe. "That only works if they have their own wish fetcher."

"Maybe. Depends."

"On what?" I asked.

"On what we do."

I gave that a short think and moved on. "Go back to your Major Planetary Thingy. Do you really reckon we could get *everyone* fed?" I asked, the issue of empty bellies being near and dear to my heart.

She set the notebook aside and leaned back on her hands. "You'd know better than I would what the limits of your wishes are. How big can we go?"

It was a sensible question. I would have liked to make a sensible reply.

"Truth to tell, I'm not really sure *how* the star power works," I admitted. "I could ask my gram."

Jura shrugged. "You don't have to. We can probably figure it out on our own."

"How's that?"

"We're dealing with stars, right? Stars mean light speed. String theory. That kind of thing." She chewed on her lip.

"So . . . when we look at the stars, the light we're seeing has been traveling for years, even centuries, before getting to Earth, right?"

I hadn't heard that, but it made some sense. "All right."

"The farther away the star, the older the starlight, right? Based on Einstein's stuff, a light from a star that's one hundred light years away took one hundred years to get here. So, if you think about it, what we're really seeing is what that star looked like one hundred years ago."

"Uh-huh."

"And when we look through a telescope at a galaxy a million light years away, we're seeing what that galaxy looked like a million years ago!"

"Bring it back around the barn, Jura."

"I'm almost there," she promised. "So. With their *really* strong telescopes, scientists can see *so* far back in time that they're actually looking at stars that were born when the universe began. Your star juice could be as infinite as the universe itself."

I was starting to get it. And, truth to tell, I was scared.

Jura grabbed my hand and shook it. "Genuine!"

"Ye-ah?"

"You have the power of the entire space-time continuum at your command!" she proclaimed. "You can go as big as you want!"

My mind reeled. I was suddenly dizzy and my shoes were

too tight. I couldn't breathe! Was that foxfire dancing before my eyes? "That's a lot of biscuits."

All right, Gen, I told myself. *Get hold of those reins. If you wanna feed the world—if you wanna be something more than Dangerous Dale Sweet's woeful daughter—big power is just what you need.*

"Good thing I've got miracle flour," I muttered.

"Miracle flour?" Jura gave me a puzzled look.

"It's this bottomless bag of flour I use to make the biscuits."

"You *are* full of surprises, Genuine Sweet."

Off in the distance, the first bell rang.

"We got three minutes." I reached for my satchel.

Jura held up her hand. "Hang on! Real quick! Let's say we did decide to end hunger. I could wish for it and you could fetch it, right? But given all the starlight infinities we're slogging through, not to mention all the steps involved in getting people organized, plus the time to grow the food—"

I saw where she was headed. "It might take a hundred years to actually make anything happen."

She nodded. "That's what I'm thinking. I mean, even my mom had to wait a few days for a job ad to appear in the *Settee,* right? If you want to make a difference—fast—we might need to find places where there's already some anti-hunger infrastructure."

"Infra-huh?"

"Places where people are already trying to get everyone fed, but maybe they don't have enough farming equipment or their government is making laws that get in the way, or something," she explained.

I flumped. "I wouldn't even know how to begin to find folks like that!"

"We don't have to. They're gonna find us!" Jura rubbed her hands together. "Ooh, this'll look *sweet* on my college application!"

She looked so excited, I hated to remind her, "We're only in the seventh grade, Jura."

"I know! Think of how far ahead of the game we'll be!" She took a pencil from behind her ear and started making notes.

Mister Strickland put on his strictest face when we walked in late.

"Nice of you to join us, Miss Sweet, Miss Carver," he said, arms folded across his chest.

"Sorry, sir," I said.

Looking all contrite, we made our way to our desks. Scree snorted a little laugh, and Sonny Wentz smiled at us as we passed by. I mean he *really* smiled.

Something odd stuck out from my desk cubby, a bit of yellow-gold paper. I eased it free to find it was a note folded in the shape of a swan. I never saw anything quite like it. On its tail was the word *Pull,* so I did.

The swan unfolded into a simple square. Written in the now-familiar writing of the chocolate giver were the words, *You bowl me over. If you feel the same, meet me at The Lanes this Saturday at two.*

Sonny Wentz had asked me out on a date! Bowling! What could be more romantic? If I were a puppy, I would've piddled myself.

8

CORNUCOPIO

THURSDAY EVENING, MY BELLY FULL OF MIRACLE-flour flapjacks, I went to meet Jura at Ham's. I was very nearly there when I caught my first glimpse of trouble.

Penny Walton had set herself in front of Ham's diner door, her arms flung open wide. Gripping her hands on either side were Missus Binset and Miz Yardley, the city clerk. Nobody could get in, including a few of Ham's regular customers, who stood nearby, gaping and confused.

Ham was there as well, waving his chili spoon and shouting—sometimes at Penny Walton, sometimes at Deputy Lamar.

"You get them out of here, Lamar, or I'll remove them myself!" Ham yelled.

"Just you try it, Ham Quimby!" Penny dared him. "I'll

pull your lease out from under you so fast your head will spin!"

I was about to saunter up and ask what the big hooray was when Penny Walton spat, "I know you're letting that Sweet girl panhandle her wishes here! Old Joe Williams couldn't gush enough about her magic! Well, let me tell you something! I am not about to let another wish fetcher finagle her way into some family's heart, just to have her turn 'round and grind their hopes under her boot heel!"

Miz Yardley cut Penny off with her own warbling protest. "No access for Sweet!"

This ruckus was about *me?*

I ducked behind a pickup truck, peeking out when I dared.

Penny Walton's daughter, Edie, tore up, hopped from her car, and started pleading with her mama to leave. "You'll strain yourself!"

Penny said something so softly I couldn't hear it, then added in a shout, "Fret over the poor families another MacIntyre wish fetcher will destroy!"

Before long, Jura appeared, crouched down at my side.

"What's going on?" she whispered.

"We can't meet at Ham's today," I said.

"They're trying to keep *you* out?"

"Looks like it," I told her.

I couldn't help noticing Deputy Lamar fingering his handcuffs. If I was the source of all this, and they saw me there, would *I* get arrested?

"Let's get out of here," I said.

"Right. Stay low." Jura slid along, her back pressed to the truck, her head below the level of the truck bed. "Be. Careful."

Grave as Jura's expression had become, I had half a mind to tell her we weren't in *that* much danger. Her life in Ardenville must have been a real upscuddle.

The crowd out in front of Ham's had grown so large that neither Penny Walton nor the deputy had a clear view of us. Quickly, but real casual-like, Jura and I crossed the street and ducked into the library.

Which, if you'll recall, was also the police department.

"Hello, ladies," a voice called out.

We jumped clear out of our skins.

Then, startled by *our* alarm, JoBeth Haines jumped clear out of hers.

"Dear goodness!" she breathed. "What has gotten into you two?"

"Sorry," I said. "We were just, uh, we —"

"May we use the Internet, Miz Haines?" Jura asked smoothly.

"I don't know . . ." JoBeth said. "Deputy Lamar just radioed in about a big ol' hoodaddy down at Ham's —"

Jura and I looked at each other.

JoBeth went on, "So you *might* want to hold off on your homework. Not often we get this kind of excitement here." A thoughtful expression crossed her face. "Not often at all. This should go in my newspaper column!" She paused again. "I don't suppose you girls could just keep an eye on things while I run across the street to get the scoop?"

"Uh, sure thing, Miz Haines," I said.

Missus Haines grabbed her notepad and rushed out the door.

And with that, we had the library to ourselves.

"Now what?" I asked Jura.

"Now . . ." She sat down in front of one of the computers and web-slung her way to whatever she was hunting.

"Now . . . I give you . . . Cornucopio!" She beamed, wafting a regal hand beneath the screen.

"Very nice," I said, taking in the various slide shows and streaming do-funnies. "What is it?"

"It's a place where people who *have* stuff connect with people who *need* stuff." She clicked and clicked once more. "Like this. Buccaneer Construction in Florida has a warehouse full of housing insulation to donate. I bet some Houses-for-Hope group is gonna snatch that right up." Click. "It's not *all* about generosity—here's a guy who just wants to trade his work truck for a sailboat—but a lot of charities do come here for help."

"Ju-ra," I said slowly. "Are we talking about the saving-the-world thing? *Now?* You do recall there may be a posse on our tail, right?"

She stopped her clicking and turned my way. "Genuine, anybody who wants to change the world is going to meet resistance. Maybe even *massive* resistance. That stuff with Penny Walton—that's a good sign! She knows you're a real agent for change! You're on the right track!"

Massive resistance? Agent for change? Wasn't it just a few weeks ago that my fondest wish was three square meals a day and an icicle-free nose in wintertime?

"Maybe we should start smaller," I suggested. "Safer."

In a distant corner of my mind, I heard Gram agree.

Jura didn't say a word. She didn't bat an eye. She just . . . waited.

A shifting reflection caught my eye, and I found myself looking at the police holding cell nearby. So many nights Pa never came home. Did he spend them there? Crazy as it might seem, I couldn't help wondering if, somehow, that might be my fate, too. Dangerous Dale's blood in my veins, *plus* the power to call down the light from the stars? What if Penny Walton was right, and I *did* manage to ruin the town somehow?

Still, it was hard to reckon why folks would be *so* riled before I'd even made my first yap-up.

I couldn't help wondering if Gram was keeping things from me. Biggish things.

Because I knew one thing for sure. Whatever it was that had people so upset, it wasn't — *it couldn't be* — wish fetching that caused it.

Jura. Missus Fuller. Chickenlady Snopes and Handyman Joe. All them bright smiles. All that sincere thanks. My wish fetching had made their lives better, not worse.

No, ma'am! I resolved. This was not Fenn, and I would *not* ruin the town! This Sass girl was gonna make good.

I took a lungful of air and let it out *real* slow.

"All right. Say a charity needed some kind of help. They'd look here for it?" I tapped the computer screen.

"Indeedy."

"And say a wish fetcher had a wish biscuit to donate. If she wanted to give it to famine relief and whatnot, she could list it on this site?"

"By George, I think she's got it!"

"Huh?"

"It's not important." Jura made crossing-out motions with her hands. "Yes. We can post a profile here, call it *Wish to End Hunger* or something, and the hunger-relief groups can contact us to make their wishes. We mail them a biscuit, and the global healing begins."

"Would it take long?" I wanted to know.

"In five minutes we could be registered and taking wish requests." She poised her hand over the mouse and waited for my signal.

"Well, if this ain't a frolic. Genuine Sweet, fourth-generation wish fetcher from tiny Sass, Georgia, goes global." I sniffed. I shook my head. I think I might have even let out a little squeak of excitement. "All right, Jura. Let's save the world!"

9

A BISCUIT FOR SCREE

LET ME TELL YOU A COUPLE THINGS ABOUT SMALL-town life. One. There ain't no such thing as secrets. Two. There ain't no such thing as sittin' fence. What do I mean by that? Just this: When I got to school the next day, two things were certain. After Penny Walton's diner ruckus, everybody would know about my wish fetching, and everybody would have some big opinion about it. I don't think there was a single time that day when the conversation didn't stop because I'd entered a room.

Sonny—my sweet Sonny—took pains to sit by me and Jura at lunch. He even went out of his way to be nice to Jura, which I thought was good of him. Martin, on the other hand, picked up his tray and left when he saw us coming. Travis was his usual lurky self, but I reckoned that didn't have much to do with wish fetching or Penny Walton.

That afternoon, Jura and I headed to the library to check Cornucopio for wish requests. Midway between here and there, Scree Hopkins turned up, sucking on a gum-pop and whispering all confidential-like.

"Genuine, is it true?" she wanted to know.

"Which part?" I asked her in the same silly whisper.

"Word has it you're conjuring ancient Cherokee power to ruin Penny Walton's real estate business!" The craziest stories always did tend to flow into Scree's pool.

"You really believe that, Scree?" I asked.

Scree shrugged. "Other folks say your granny used to grant wishes sometimes, and now you're taking after her. Some say it's a mighty fine thing you're doing."

"Well, that stuff is true," Jura said.

"It is?" Scree's eyes went wide with pleading.

I sighed. "Something I can do for you, Scree?"

She launched like a hawk on a mouse. "Well, you know how my Micky turns sixteen next week? And how times have been so hard for the Forkses since the saw shop closed? Well, Micky really, *really* wants a car. Maybe even a *new* car. And there's no *possible* way he can get it for himself, what with all his work money going to his family. So, what I was wondering is, do you think you could wish him up a car?"

I'll tell you straight-up, I didn't want to do it. I had no

problem granting wishes for things people *needed*, like food. And really, I was all right with fetching certain things they might *want*, like a long-lost army medal. But frivolous things, things that bordered on pure selfishness? I did not at all relish the idea of wish-fetching a vehicle just so Scree could have the pleasure of being driven through town in her boyfriend's new car.

But there was one thing that kept me from refusing her flat out. It was common knowledge that Micky Forks dreamed of becoming a stock-car racer someday. He longed for it the way I longed to keep my kin fed and warm. And it was true, with all his money going to the family bailout, the chances of him saving enough to buy a car were downright minuscule.

It wouldn't cost me nothin' but a biscuit to set him on the road to his dream.

While I was thinking this through, Jura leaned over and whispered in my ear. "Probably better to have Gossip Girl on our side, especially with Penny Walton's bad press."

I looked at her. Jura nodded sagely.

"All right, Scree," I said. "One new car for Micky."

She squealed so long and so hard I thought she might be having a fit.

Quick as I could, I whispered her wish to a biscuit so I could shove it in her mouth and stop the din.

"Oh, Genuine! Thank you! I'll never forget it!" Scree

exclaimed, though her mouth was half full. And off she ran in the direction of Micky's house.

Out west, over the mountains, lightning flashed. A storm was brewing.

All at once, I got an uneasy feeling.

JoBeth Haines raised an eyebrow when Jura and I swung open the library door, but when I asked if we might use the computer, JoBeth only smiled and told us to help ourselves.

Jura logged us in to Cornucopio, and I scooted my chair up next to hers, eager to see what wishes had arrived. Folks didn't seem to understand we were serious. In twenty-four hours, all's we had were three replies: a message saying if we wanted to play pranks, we should do it on SmoochBook, and two pukish wish requests I won't bother to repeat.

Jura put the filters on after that, but otherwise, she wasn't worried in the least.

"By the way," she said, "I used my aunt's number as the phone contact. You know, just in case yours gets disconnected by mistake."

Just in case the bill doesn't get paid is what she meant. As much as it pained me to admit it, it was a sensible arrangement.

"That's fine. They're not exactly storming the barn doors, anyway. How are we supposed to save the world if no one makes a wish?" I asked.

"Easy," she told me. "*I wish* that the groups who can best end world hunger will find our profile and make legitimate wish requests."

"Huh," I chuckled. "I guess I'm bakin' you a wish biscuit tonight."

When I got home, I found a letter addressed to me from the electric company:

Rumpp County Power
26 Wexler Street
Pitney, GA 39902

Dear Ms. Sweet:

Thank you for your letter regarding payment of your electric bill. Unfortunately, we do not accept payment in the form of goods and/or services. For your convenience, you may pay your bill with cash, check, or credit card. Our offices are open 9 a.m. to 5 p.m., Monday through Friday.

Please note your current bill is three days overdue.

Sincerely,

Abernathy Hoist
Account Representative

I frowned at it, but not for long. Why worry over something that I couldn't do anything about—at least until the office opened on Monday? I put the letter back in the envelope and set it under the living room lamp.

10

AWFUL, WONDERFUL

SATURDAY MORNING CAME, AND THE WORLD WAS
sunshine and light once again. It's a fine thing, what
a good night's sleep can do for you.

Course, it also might have had something to do with the
fact that, in less than seven hours, I'd be meeting Sonny for
our first date.

That's right. This was *the* Saturday, bowling day, the day
I'd decreed as Love on the Lanes Day.

But by lunchtime, my heebie-jeebies had gobbled up my
hip-hoorays. I was so nervous I barely made it through my
egg salad sandwich. After that, I spent half an hour trying on
all the clothes I owned, only to discover that they were all
downright horrible. Unlovely as I felt, I started to wonder if
Sonny's asking me out would turn out to be some big joke at
my expense.

"You all right, Gen?" Gram stood in the bathroom door-way, a fist on her hip.

The shower curtain rod was strewn with pants and tops, a skirt, and my two dresses.

I slumped. "Gram, a boy asked me to go bowling, but I don't think I can go. If it ain't bad enough that I'm homely, my clothes are so tired a thrift store wouldn't take 'em."

"Oh, honey." Gram put a hand on my cheek. "You're not homely. You're just growing. You look the way your ma did at your age." I knew for a fact Gram had always regarded my ma as quite beautiful. "As for your clothes, well, I will admit they need some freshening up. I'll tell you what. Give me that yella top, there. You put on your jeans, and get the rest of that mess folded up and put away."

I gave her the top. There wasn't much to it. It was a plain, button-down, collared shirt.

An hour later, Gram found me staring at the TV—Chef Guy's *Holy Crepe!* She sat down next to me and set the shirt in my lap.

The top's plain plastic buttons had been replaced with mother-of-pearl ones, ringed in silver. The corners of my collar were fancied with pointed silver tips. It was simple and elegant, but not too showy for the bowling alley. Gram hadn't done much, but what she had done made all the difference.

I jumped and jiggled and hugged Gram all at the same time, which must have been a sight.

Gram laughed. "I guess you like it."

"I do! It's perfect! Where'd you get these?" I touched the buttons and the collar tips.

"Aw, they was just lying around," she replied. "Now, how long till you meet your young man? Do you have time for me to do your hair?"

I did. Gram plugged in her old curling iron and gave my hair "just a little body," as she called it. In five minutes, I had curls where there weren't any before. I grinned at the mirror, feeling like the prize peacock.

"Now, don't kiss on the first date!" Gram shouted out the front door as I was leaving. "And if he tries anything you don't like, you have your gram's own permission to bite him. Hard! All right?"

I hear you city folk have these twenty-lane bowl-a-ramas with glow-in-the-dark paint and loud music and such. The Lanes isn't anything like that. In fact, one lane fewer, and they'd have had to call it The Lane. There's one pair of bowling shoes for each size, except the men's elevens and the women's sevens, of which there are two pair. The grill offers swivel-stool seating for four, as well as a selection of burgers (with cheese, without, with pickle, without) and the world's best, greasiest, make-you-mildly-ill-after-you-eat-'em french fries. Let me tell you, one day at lunch, stop in. They're worth the bellyache.

I pulled up a stool and looked at the clock. Five minutes

to two. Five minutes to get myself together. Or to worry, which is what I actually I did.

Why did Gram have to mention that kissing thing? I mean, really, wasn't that something that was best left unplanned and natural-like? Now I'd be thinking about it the whole time. Would Sonny try to kiss me? And if he did, what should I do? Kiss him back? Slap him? Run? I supposed I could always bite him, as Gram had suggested. I couldn't help laughing a little at that thought.

"Hello, Genuine. It's a genuine pleasure to see you today."

My vision of me kissing—or biting—Sonny popped like a balloon. Beside me stood Travis Tromp, dressed all in black except that—*oh, no!*—his shirt had mother-of-pearl buttons and silver collar tips.

"May I join you?" His words came out strangely, like he'd memorized and practiced them.

"Suit yourself," I said, looking out the window to see if Sonny was coming.

"My ma sends her regards," Travis said.

This did catch my interest a mite. "How's she doing? Is she seeing anyone?" I figured probably not yet, as my vegetables hadn't started arriving.

"Not so far, but don't you doubt it, Genuine, she's a believer." His face brightened, and he looked a little less dreary. "I am, too. Ma told me about your wish fetching. I always suspected you was a little magical."

"That makes one of us," I said. "But life does surprise sometimes."

He nodded. "Sure does. I didn't think you were gonna come today."

"What do you mean?" I asked, glancing at the door.

"I was pretty sure you hated me."

"Not *hate*," I replied.

"But my ma said, 'What can it hurt, just to ask her?' The chocolate was her idea. Did you like it? I don't eat much candy myself."

I froze. "I'm sorry. What?"

"Candy. Chocolate and butterscotch and such. This one Easter, though—"

"Are you telling me that chocolate was from *you?*" My voice shook.

"Shore."

"*You* invited me bowling today?"

"Who'd you think?" He smiled a little sideways.

I moaned. "Sonny Wentz!"

His smile vanished.

"I should have known." He took a deep, sort-of ragged breath and spoke through gritted teeth. "Will you excuse me for a minute, Genuine?" He didn't wait for me to answer before he disappeared into the men's room.

Travis Tromp! I was on a date with Mister Blackpants Blackshirt Blackington! My gut wrenched. My cheeks burned.

How could I have been such a fool as to think Sonny Wentz would ask out bucktoothed, freckle-faced Genuine Sweet? The daughter of Dangerous Dale! I was so embarrassed, I considered very seriously crawling down into a pin sweep at the end of the lanes and letting it brush me into whatever dusty cubby lay beyond.

"Surely no one would find me there," I muttered.

Nearby, Travis cleared his throat. "Genuine."

"What?" I said it rudely, I admit.

"I think it's fair to say we're both disappointed," he said, still measuring his words. "But why don't we make the best of it? Let's at least play a game or two. As friends."

I looked at the floppy hair hanging into his eyes, his over-sized ears, the weird boot chain around the ankle of his Converse shoe — and I couldn't help thinking of Jura saying how she was like him.

I sighed. "Yeah. All right."

He gave a sharp, almost dignified nod. "All right, then. What size shoe you wear? It's on me."

It was curious that a game of tenpins would inspire Travis so, but jokes started rolling off that boy's tongue like comedy was his calling. He laughed. He capered. Once he even spun me in a two-step! Plus, he said "Thank you"—and *smiled*—when Miz B., the alley owner, came to clear out our yapped-up ball return. Outside of school, the boy was, well, downright likable.

By the end of the first round, I was losing badly but enjoying myself all the same. "You may have won the battle, but I"—I thumped my chest—"I shall win the war!"

Travis laughed. "Best two out of three?"

"Think you're man enough?" I teased.

"Think you're woman enough?" he retorted, raising an eyebrow.

"Just watch me." I sashayed up to the lane and rolled my ball—right into the gutter. Twice.

Travis hefted his bowling ball. "What did you say right then? Something about winning the war?"

"You'll see! I'm lying in wait. Crouched in the underbrush, fixin' to spring," I assured him.

And then I lost so soundly—not once, but three whole times—that Miz B. came and took the ball right out of my hand.

"This ain't your game, Genuine," she said gently.

"It ain't that bad," Travis defended me.

"It wounds me just to watch her!" said Miz B. "Y'all come have some fries on the house, then get out of here. Leagues are coming in at four."

It was hard to argue with free fries, so we sat ourselves down and ate until we ailed slightly.

"These are awful," Travis whispered.

"Awfully wonderful," I replied.

He nodded his queasy agreement.

Drawing a floppy fry through his ketchup-mustard swirl, Travis said, "Want to hang out again sometime? As friends?"

"Um. All right. Sure." Truth to tell, I'd had a really good time. "As friends."

When I got home, Gram asked me how things had gone with my young man. I wasn't sure what to say. If I admitted I'd had a good time, she might want to invite Travis over, which could give him the wrong idea. On the other hand, if I told her about the mix-up, she might hunt down Sonny Wentz and thrash him for hurting my feelings.

I finally settled on, "Our buttons and collar tabs matched. He didn't try to kiss me."

"That's . . . promising, I reckon." She reached into her sewing bag for a new ball of yarn. "By the by, your new friend, Jura, stopped by to pick up that biscuit you left for her. And she wants you to meet her at the library tomorrow. Something about a cornucopia. Says you should get set for a busy week," Gram told me.

"A cornucopia?" It took me a minute. "Oh! Cornucopio!"

"What on earth's that?" Gram asked.

"It's a thing with profiles and swaps. And college applications, for Jura, at least." I bit my lip. Maybe now was the time to tell her about our plans to feed the world. "To be honest—"

"College, huh?" Gram mused. "I don't know but what the smart ones always have some sort of big plan. Well, good for her, I say. Not enough big plans in Sass, of late."

"No. Right. You're exactly right. Which brings me to—"

"You don't mind if I turn in early, do you, Gen? I worked myself to the bone today."

I looked at the clock. "It's not even five."

"Old people tucker out fast."

And with that, she shuffled off to her room.

She'd left me a frittata in the skillet, still warm, so I helped myself. After a little homework, I grabbed my starlight cup and headed into the woods.

It was a Saturday night, so the older kids were out being rowdy. I could hear them in the distance hooting and laughing, engines revving and tires a-squealing. It was all the usual business, and I was used to it, so it wasn't hard to put it out of mind.

The air was a little cool. Winter'd be upon us before long, and I remembered I still had to figure a way to negotiate with the power company. It was one thing to trade for wishes with a person, but businesses, I guess, didn't have spots in their ledgers for payments in wish biscuits.

Wasn't long before I forgot about that, too, though. The stars shone so brightly, and even the white wisps of the Milky

Way were on display if you relaxed your eyes and let yourself take it all in. I was standing that way, looking but not exactly staring, when I thought I heard something like a song.

I reckoned it might be the high schoolers fooling around, but no, it wasn't. The Fort brothers never belched out a sound like this. It was high and sweet, and a little tricky, so I couldn't be sure I'd really heard anything at all.

I plugged my ears with my fingers to see if it was something coming from inside my own head, but the sound disappeared until I unplugged them again.

"Hello?" I called into the night.

The song didn't stop, but I thought it might have grown just a little louder. And maybe—were those *words?* Sometimes it seemed they were, and sometimes it seemed the words were my name. But when I tried to listen harder, it wasn't my name at all. It was something else. Bells. Or a sound like the metal triangle the drummer plays in band, but constant, a single, long ringing, so high and silvery it wasn't quite real.

It was coming from the sky, I realized.

The stars were singing.

For a while, I could only listen. But then, as the music swirled and grew, I couldn't help opening my own mouth and trying to sing along. And I'll tell you what, I am no singer, but it seemed to me, in that starlit clearing, that my voice suited that music just perfectly, and I knew the words to the song, even though I couldn't hear them with my ears, precisely.

All shall be well and all shall be well
and all manner of thing shall be well . . .

And everything *was* well. Electricity or no. Pa, drunk or sober. For just that moment, I felt safe and content. I felt one other thing, too: my ma was there, and somehow, she was hugging me and loving me through that song.

I'm not ashamed to admit I cried a little. But it wasn't because she was gone and I missed her. It was because she was there, right there, and—in a way I didn't quite under-stand—she always had been.

There came a time that it felt right to raise my cup and whistle down some magic from the stars. It was then that I realized: the light *was* the song, which *was* the light. It was more than that, too, but *what* more, I couldn't fathom. It was a mystery far bigger than me.

And you know what? I took a great deal of comfort from that.

After I made a double batch of wish biscuits—an especially fine-looking bunch, if I say so myself—I used the last of the starlight to light the stove for a batch of plain old breakfast biscuits. I couldn't help feeling pleased as I tucked them in the breadbasket and folded the cloth over them. Having those biscuits made would save Gram a little work in the morning.

The bag of miracle flour was as full as it had been when I first brought it home.

11

EL LIZARD PRIMARO

ONE OF THE NICE THINGS ABOUT THE PUBLIC library sharing a building with the Sass Police Department is, even if the librarian goes home, the library itself is never closed. True, it's no fun having to do your studying in full view of a holding cell where a certain town drunkard might be sleeping it off, but every rose has a few thorns.

Jura was there when I arrived.

"So-o?" She pushed her face at me and fluttered her lashes.

I laughed. " 'So' what?"

"Yesterday! Your date!"

I'd told her about the notes from Travis, of course, though at the time I'd thought they were from Sonny. Now the whole thing was just embarrassing.

I fessed up.

"Travis!" Jura exclaimed. A look of concern crossed her face. "You were nice about it, weren't you?"

"Nice? I bowled three games with him!"

She gave me an approving nod. "Good for you." Then she added, "So, *was* it? A date?"

"Course not. I was real clear. Friends only." I felt my cheeks turn red. "Could we get down to business?"

A little smile played on Jura's lips, but she took her place before the computer and signed us in to Cornucopio. "Okay. Let's see what we've got."

She frowned at the screen.

"Ho-ho-ho-ly Christmas," was what she finally said.

"What? What?"

She turned the screen my way and tapped on it. It read, *Welcome,* **Wish to End Hunger.** *You have* **74** *new messages.*

We clicked. We read. We clicked again and read some more. They were—every single one of 'em—real wish requests. Folks wrote us from as far away as Russia and as close as Ardenville, Georgia. We heard from tiny efforts operating out of garages and mega-outfits that were working to feed continents.

Dear Wish to End Hunger, one message began. *We know your posting is probably a prank, but after hundreds of layoffs in our community, we're not too proud to hope for a little magic.*

Dear WTEH, said another. *We've got plenty of non-*

perishable food, but no way to deliver it to remote mountain families. If we don't get truck repairs and volunteers fast, people are going to starve this winter. If there is anything you can do, magic or otherwise, PLEASE HELP.

That one was fairly worrying, but the next message tore me up something awful.

It said, *Last month in our village, three children and one elder died of hunger. If we do not have help, we expect at least fifteen others will die before the year's end.*

My knees threatened to buckle. Four people dead of hunger! Three of 'em kids like me! And an elder who could have been somebody's gram, as precious as my own and loved just as fiercely.

And there were so many more.

"I don't think I made enough biscuits last night," I said softly.

Jura gaped. "This is . . . wow. This is intense."

That afternoon, Jura and I picked out our first eight wishes—because that's how many biscuits I had made. Then I whispered to the bread, staying faithful to the wishers' requests—after all, they knew what they needed far better than I ever could.

With sixty-six wishes remaining, I brought a bucket that night, rather than a cup, to hold all the starlight. The stars obliged and filled it to the brim. Thanks to Dilly's flour, I had more than enough fixin's, but it was nearly daybust before I finished baking all that dough.

Jura met me at my house on Monday morning. From there, we went to the post office, where a little pre-planning — by which I mean a biscuit held back for a certain purpose — paid off.

"There's just no way I can give you free boxes and postage," Postmaster Marion said, her face squinched with regret. "I'd get in terrible trouble. I wish I could help you."

Did somebody say *wish?*

"Miss Marion, have you eaten breakfast yet?" I asked.

"Why, now that you mention it, I've been so busy since the truck came in, I haven't had a chance."

Jura pulled a biscuit from her purse and wafted it under Marion's nose. "Have you heard about Genuine's dee-licious biscuits?"

"I might have," Marion admitted. "Is that . . . one of 'em?"

I whispered Marion's wish to the biscuit and offered it to her. Two minutes after her last mouthful, the phone rang. Marion answered it.

"Yes, ma'am," she said to the caller. "Yes, ma'am. I surely will, ma'am. You, too. Goodbye." She hung up the phone.

"You already know what I'm going to say, don't you?" Marion asked.

"We got our boxes and stamps," I replied.

"Headquarters wants all the postmasters to choose a local charity and cover their shipping costs, postage, boxes—everything down to the last scrap of packing tape. Some new public affairs campaign." Marion gave her head a shake. "Looks like I choose you two."

Some butt-waggling victory dancing followed, but not too much. We had important biscuits to ship.

At homeroom, Jura showed up at my desk with a stack of papers printed off the school computer. Forty-three new wish requests.

Another twenty-six came in before lunch.

There were eighty, total, by the time the last bell rang. I was in for another sleepless night.

That evening, Gram watched from the kitchen table as I darted between the raindrops, bringing in my second bucket of starlight.

"My goodness, Gen. You starting a factory operation?" She picked up a rolling pin and started kneading flour.

"Something like that," I replied, surly with weariness.

"Anything I should know about?"

I shrugged.

I could tell she was aiming for a more satisfying reply. When I didn't offer one, she only said, "Hope they don't go bad before you use 'em all. Though the magic *might* keep 'em fresh. Even after all these years, I still don't know what all that starlight's capable of."

Surely I should have told her about Wish to End Hunger right then, but with last night's lack of sleep *and* the promise of a long night in front of me, it just seemed easier to hold off.

"There's peach cider, if you want some," I mumbled instead. "Mister Cortez brought it in trade for a wish that he could get rid of a tune that's been stuck in his head."

"And did he?"

"About six seconds after he ate his wish biscuit."

Gram's voice seemed a little far away as she said, "That's real fine."

After a time, she added, "Gen?"

I didn't take my eyes off my work, but said, "Yeah, Gram?"

There came a long pause.

"It can wait. You're busy."

Gram turned in around nine that night, but I was still making biscuits long past two. I was so dog-tired as I staggered from the kitchen that I accidentally knocked the miracle flour off the counter, sending a huge puff of it into the air and all across the floor. It took me another thirty minutes to clean up the mess I'd made.

* * *

After my second straight night of biscuit baking, with no more than three hours' sleep under my belt, I stumbled off to school. There I found Jura at her desk, all serenity and poise, surrounded by no less than a dozen people. Their voices were raised, and it was a bit of a scrum, but they weren't angry. They were wishin'.

"I'll give my whole rock collection if Genuine can wish-fetch Mister Tabbypants home!" said Didi Orr, Martin's little sister.

Jura noted this down.

"Here's what I need: sixteen two-by-fours, a big box of nails, some tar, and a can of paint," said Dennis Talley, a senior.

"What do you have to trade?" Jura asked. "Genuine takes trades."

"Any kind of chores, I'll do. Repairs and honey-dos and stuff, not scrubbin' toilets, mind."

"No toilets," Jura noted, and looked up and saw me. "There's the woman of the hour." She smiled.

Everyone turned.

A chorus of voices shouted, "Genuine! Could you please—? Can you just—? You have to—!" The rest got lost in the scut and scuffle.

"Back off, people!" Jura shouted. "I've got everyone's requests right here. She can't do anything for you until school's out for the day. Come on! At least let her put down her backpack!"

I did put down my backpack. Then I tripped over it trying to get to my chair. The chair bumped my desk, knocking all my pencils from the cubby. As I crawled around trying to collect them, I hit my head on the sharp edge of the plastic chair — though I was so exhausted it didn't occur to me that I might be bleeding. When I looked up again, the entire seventh grade, not to mention all the would-be wishers, were gawping at me.

Thankfully, Mister Strickland appeared and shooed the other-graders from the room.

"Not turning our classroom into a wish-fetcher outpost, are we, ladies?" he asked.

"No, sir," we both replied. Jura quickly tucked the wish list into her purse.

When Mister Strickland disappeared into the supply closet, I grabbed Jura's sleeve and gave it a sleepy tug.

"Jura, I don't know how many more biscuits I can bake —"

"I know, but with Scree Hopkins running through the halls bragging about Micky's new car, I had to do something to stop the stampede! I thought if I made it barter-only, it might discourage a few people. And, if not, you'd at least get a warm winter coat and some house chores for your effort," she said.

"Micky got his car?" I knew he would, but it still came as a shock to hear it for real.

Jura nodded. "A *brand-new* car. From a stock-car racing scholarship Micky *never applied for.*"

Sonny walked in just then and gave Jura and me a glance. His cheeks flared red. It didn't detract one iota from his good looks.

"Wonder what that's about?" I mused.

Mister Strickland reappeared and swatted his desk with a pointer. "If you're finished with your conversations, folks, can we get a little work done?"

The lunchroom was a madhouse. Everyone wanted something, and they wouldn't leave us be till they saw their names on that wish list. Finally, Jura couldn't keep up with the requests. Though my eyes blurred with fatigue and my hand trembled in exhaustion, I tore out my own scrap of paper and started writing, too.

While I was noting down that Donut was willing to barter his junior detective skills (who knew?) for his very own milk goat, a hand settled onto my shoulder.

"Hey, Genuine." It was Travis.

The crowd actually parted. A great silence fell, and I couldn't help feeling it was because they were waiting to see what zinger the new queen of Sass, fourth-generation wish fetcher, would deliver.

Now, here was the thing. Travis and I had sort of crossed a line on Saturday, almost like we were real friends. It wouldn't be right to neglect him, and I really didn't want to. But there was this whole "Travis is a jerk" thing to deal with. And he *was*— he *really* was—to other people. So I couldn't just ask him to pull up a chair, either.

Something warred in me right then. That day in the lunchroom was the most attention I'd ever received in my whole life. The older kids, who I usually looked on with a certain amount of trepidation, were talking to me like I was an actual person, and I could tell that the other seventh-graders were basking like lizards in the reflected light. Well, call me *el lizard primaro*, because I surely wanted to keep that white-hot spotlight of adulation shining brightly down. And Travis, well, what could he do but dim the beam, if you take my meaning?

I don't owe him anything, I thought. *I didn't ask him out. I didn't hide who I was until the last possible second.*

No, but I did let him pay for my bowling shoes. And I did tell him I wanted to hang out again sometime. If I deny him now, I'd be nothing but a fair-weather friend.

So what? What does that even mean, "fair-weather friend"?

I noticed that Jura was giving me a look of such trust and faith, her eyes practically shone with it.

"Can you handle things for a minute?" I asked her.

"Sure," she replied.

I got up and left the table with Travis.

Inevitably, we were followed by various *woo-hoo*s, cat whistles, and even a lame *hubba-hubba*.

"What's up, Travis?" I was feeling irritable and I heard it in my voice. Taking a deep breath, I reminded myself that—even if he'd made himself a nuisance for the last couple years and had thoroughly earned all the dislike that me and the other kids hurled at him—Travis was now, sort of, my friend.

"I was wondering if you might want to go bowling Saturday." He drummed his thumbs on his hips.

"Could you stop that?" I said.

"What?"

"Never mind." I yawned, and then managed to lift my head enough to look him in the eye. "I can't go out this weekend, Travis. Sorry."

"You on restriction or something?"

I shook my head.

"Changed your mind about being friends, I guess." He started to walk away.

I wasn't feeling coordinated enough to chase him, so I let out a pitiful, "Tra-vis!"

"Yeah?"

"Look at me."

He looked.

"Do I seem healthy to you? Well rested?"

He stepped up to me and got a little closer than I might normally have allowed.

"I guess you don't." He set a hand on my shoulder. "You all right, Genuine?"

"No! I been up for two nights in a row baking wish biscuits. And I'll be baking till dawn again tonight, because I can't even *start* collecting starlight till the sun goes down. I am tireder than a three-legged dog in a roomful of rocking chairs." Wait. Did that make sense? "No bowling. Saturday and Sunday, I have one thing on my calendar, Travis. Sleep!"

"Genuine!" Jura appeared. "It's almost one o'clock!"

Dangit! If we didn't get the new batch of biscuits to the post office before lunchtime was over, we'd miss the daily pickup.

"I don't suppose it could wait till tomorrow," I said. But of course it couldn't. People could starve.

I could see Jura considering the dark smears under my eyes. "Never mind. I'll take care of all the shipping. That'll be my job from now on. You just bake the biscuits and whisper the wishes into them." She paused. "And, uh, speaking of biscuits . . ."

She held up a few printed pages.

"No!" I protested.

She sighed. "There can't be many more anti-hunger groups in the world. I bet if we make it through the weekend, things will slow down."

"I'm so *tired*, Jura."

"You're fetching wishes to feed hungry people?" Travis asked.

"Yes." My chin dropped to my chest.

We three stood there, quiet for a time. Then the lunch-room door swung open and Tray Daynor saw me standing there.

"Here she is!" he shouted.

A dozen students poured through the cafeteria doors, every one of them calling my name.

"All right." Travis gave a purposeful nod. "Jura, you and me, let's get those biscuits to the post office. Genuine, you tell Strickland you're going home sick, get a little rest if you can. I'll see you at eight."

"Eight," I agreed.

He could have said, "Go get a little rest and the chicken dance is at eight." It would have held as much meaning for me right then. I didn't even remember to tell the teacher I was leaving. I just ducked into a classroom, climbed out the window, and, like a tired balloon, drifted sideways home.

12

A GLINT OF SILVER

NIGHT FELL, AND I HADN'T GOTTEN NEARLY enough rest.

Bucket of starlight in my arms, I plodded my way through pure mud. Twice I stumbled over tree roots. My hair tangled in some low-hanging branches. When I finally got back to the house, I found Pa passed out drunk on the sofa.

No!

Even if I could get all the biscuits done before three or so, I'd *still* have to chase him into his own bed. I was too *tired* to rouse him. Too *tired* for his flailing arms and mean-spirited, muttered complaints.

I flumped to the floor and began to cry.

"Genuine?" a voice came from the open doorway.

I turned around. "Hey, Travis." With a big sniffle, I added, "I ain't cryin'."

"I can see that." He helped me up.

"Gram's the one who can always get him to move, but she's asleep already," I told him.

Travis glanced at Dangerous Dale. "You want him in there?" he asked, hitching a thumb toward Pa's room.

I nodded.

"Tell you what," he said. "You get started on those biscuits. But tell me what you're doing as you go, all right? I'll move your pa."

I was too bone-weary to fathom it at the time, but Travis took all of Pa's grumblings and thrashings upon himself and got my father into his own bed in record time.

I was still mixing dough when Travis came into the kitchen.

"What are you doing now?"

"Stirrin'," I said.

Fortunately, he was a better observer than I was an explainer.

"So, about one cup of wish juice to every two cups of flour?" he asked.

"Guess so." By now, I was mostly doing it by instinct.

"And how long you bake 'em for?"

"Until they look right," I replied.

He waited for me to pull the first batch from the oven and gave them a real careful looking over.

"And that's all?"

"That's all till I whisper to 'em," I said.

"But you don't have to do that right away? That can wait until morning?"

I yawned. "Yup."

"Good." He set his hands on my shoulders and walked me to the sofa. "Lie down. Sleep."

"I can't," I whined. "Starving people. Biscuits."

"I'll make the biscuits. You sleep."

"You can't—"

"I can, too. My ma's a chef. Don't worry." He gently set his foot behind my heels and gave me a karate sweep right back onto the sofa.

"Hey!"

"Good night, Genuine."

The fight went out of me as soon as I hit the pillow.

"Night, Trav's."

Just after dawn, I woke to find these things: Pa quietly shut up in his room. Gram humming over a skillet of scrambled eggs. Seventy-two wish biscuits wrapped in a towel and set in a laundry basket. And the stack of yesterday's wish requests, each one with the particular wish highlighted in yellow.

There was also a note:

Your oven's real small. Come to my house and we'll

use my ma's big one. Bet we can make it so you're

asleep by ten. —T

The following day, Jura and I used our every free moment to try to sort through our wish lists. I say "try" because, each time we started to get down to it, some other-grader would come in to tell us something else they needed.

Ham was waiting for us outside of school after the last bell.

"Genuine," he pleaded, "I can't get them to leave. Could you please come to the diner and help me move 'em along?"

I knew what I'd find when I got there: Penny Walton and the entire Sass Women's Club, every one of them shrieking and pointing fingers. I didn't want to go, but I couldn't leave them to ruin Ham's business, either.

"I'll come right now," I told him.

"Not without me, you're not," Jura said.

Even from down the way and across the street, I could see that Ham's was sardine-packed. A row of people stood at the door and curled around the side of the building.

Ham used his bulk to shuffle me and Jura through the door. There was a slew of familiar faces there, but Penny Walton wasn't among them.

"All right, folks! She's here!" Ham hollered. He led me to "my" booth, where I'd given Miz Tromp and Handyman Joe

their wish biscuits. Cousin Faye stood nearby, just a-beamin'
as she taped a construction-paper sign to the table:

Reserved! for
Sass's Own
Genuine Sweet,
Wish Fetcher

Jura and I slid into the booth. What else *could* we do?
One by one, the citizens of Sass came forward, some hopeful
and some pained, but all of them with a wish that needed
fetching.

If only their faces weren't so full of trust. If only they'd
ask for things like jewels and TVs, instead of medicine and
work clothes, I could send 'em packing. Instead, I tore page
after page from my notebook, taking it all down, watching as
the number of wish biscuits I'd need to make doubled, then
tripled.

Dimly, I recalled the ghost in *Macbeth* who said, "Sleep
no more!"

I caught my mirror image in the window and pondered
what it might be like to live *there,* on the distant side of things.
Folks couldn't demand doodly from me; I'd be nothing but a
reflection, far away, where things were watery and quiet. For
a time, I just lingered there in my imagination.

As if from far off, I heard Jura talking with Jerry Tatum about a tractor.

"It don't have to be new. I'd take just about any tractor, long as it ran." He shrugged. "Course I can't pay for it."

"No, I understand," Jura replied, "but maybe you have something you can trade?"

"Well, I ain't got no crops for trade, 'cause I ain't got no tractor."

"No, I can see that," Jura agreed. "But there must be something—a service maybe?"

He couldn't think of anything.

"Genuine? Any ideas?" Jura asked me.

From the stack of wish lists, a twinkle caught my eye. Silver light danced beside one of the names. Missus Sandidge had wished for a place to hold her twenty-fifth annual family reunion. A few notes of otherworldly music rang in my ear. I knew that song! It was the melody of the stars!

"Mister Tatum, that big barn of yours, the one facing the Henderson property, is it still empty?" I asked, starting to get excited.

"'Cept for my dead tractor," he answered.

"Would you be willing to let someone use that barn for just a few days, if they would *loan* you their tractor when they weren't using it?" I knew the Sandidges had a fine tractor that they used for only part of one season each year.

He nodded so broadly it nearly doubled him over. "Heck, yes!"

Missus Sandidge was still at Ham's counter slurping a milkshake. I called her over. In under sixty seconds, both Jerry and Missus Sandidge left smiling.

"You're a genius, Genuine!" Jura exclaimed. "That's two less biscuits you have to bake! Who else can we pair up?"

By six-thirty, Ham's place had cleared out.

"Mister Rucker," I said into Ham's phone, "if you'll see Miz Sams in the morning, I know she'd love to swap you some housecleaning help in exchange for a ride to her doctor appointment in Ardenville."

Jura called Dennis Talley. "The hardware store needs an extra hand over the holidays, Dennis. They can't afford wages, but they'll be happy to pay you in building materials."

And so it went. By eight o'clock, we had paired fourteen additional sets of people.

Hanging up the phone, Jura turned to me. "Not bad for a day's work."

"Miz Sams was really excited." I had to smile.

"They all were," Jura agreed.

"Genuine Sweet! What were you thinking?" Gram met me at the gate. She held her hands in a knot at her chest.

"Roxie Fuller showed me on her computer what you

done," she fretted. "Saying you're a fourth-generation wish fetcher! From Sass, Georgia, no less! Putting up your picture for all the world to see!"

I gaped. "But Gram! You said Ma advertised in the Ardenville newspaper!"

"She didn't put her name! And she used one of those blind addresses! Nobody ever knew who she was!" She plunked down on Pa's apple crate and put her head in her hands.

Gazing up at me, her eyes full of regret, she said, "I didn't even think to remember you might put your wishes on those Interwebs."

"But . . . you said to find my own way," I reminded her.

"And here's what comes of it." She held out her hand, revealing a balled-up paper. I smoothed it open against my palm.

Now Hiring, the flyer said. *Town Handyman. Apply at City Hall.*

"This is something Pa might be able to do!" I exclaimed. "Don't you think?"

"I did think so," Gram agreed. "Even went to city hall to get the details."

I gulped. "And?"

"And I run into Penny Walton." Gram took the job ad from me. "She told me Dale shouldn't bother to apply—not while his daughter's running around making trouble like she is."

"No!"

"I asked her what business it was of hers—she don't run this town. She said the mayor wouldn't dare hire against her wishes, seeing as how he's hoping to buy one of her properties for a real low price. Can you believe that? Full-out bribery! The very stench of it!"

I was strack hard. That job could have made a real difference for us. Bills paid. Groceries bought. Penny Walton making a ruckus on the street corner was one thing, but this was real spite—the dangerous sort.

"Why is she doing this? I don't understand."

Gram looked away. "There's nothin' to understand. Penny's just mad, doin' what mad people do."

"This goes *way* past mad! Gram, please! Don't send me to the cotillion without eye shadow! You have got to tell me why she is so riled!"

She was quiet for a time. "All right, Gen. I expect if I don't tell you, someone else will."

My heart did a double thump. Now that I'd asked for the truth, I wasn't at all sure I wanted to hear it.

I cowgirled up. "I'm listening."

She looked at me, still standing there holding the wish lists under my arm. "Sit, honey. You're making me nervous."

I sat down, facing her, with my back against one of our termite-chewed porch beams.

"So, what happened is," Gram began, "some trouble came up. With some people. And there was some hurt feelings and some folks got mad. Then there was a sad to-do, but time passed and now, for the most part, it's done with." She gave me a fuzzy little half-smile. "You see?"

"I . . . think I'm gonna need a few more details," I said.

"Right. Course you will." She smoothed her skirt. And started picking lint off it. Then she took off her glasses and started cleaning them on her shirt.

"Gram!"

"All right!" She swatted the tops of her legs. "What I said about your ma, her fetching anonymous wishes through a newspaper ad, that was all true. Cristabel kept things real quiet. But that didn't stop people in Sass from putting two and two together. My ma was a fetcher, I was a fetcher, so, of course—"

"Everyone in town figured Ma was a wish fetcher, too," I ventured.

"Exactly," Gram agreed. "And folks started coming to her for wishes. But she always turned them away, telling 'em *I* was the Sass wish fetcher, and if they wanted something, *I* was the MacIntyre to see.

"Except this one time.

"See, Cristabel and Penny Walton used to run together, real good friends, and Penny's big sister, Loreen, had taken ill." Gram's eyes darted away. "It was bad. Lot of pain. And what with Cristabel spending so much of her time with Penny, she saw the very worst of it, up-close. So, one day, when Penny broke into tears, wishing for all the world that Loreen would get better, your ma said, 'Let's see what we can do.'"

It was hard to imagine a time when Penny Walton had anything but ire for my kin and our wishes. "And Penny let her?"

"Let her? Begged her, is more like," Gram said. "So, Cristabel went into Loreen's room, all alone, and spoke with her for a time. And . . . something happened."

"What?" I asked.

Gram shook her head. "Cristabel would never tell me. Nor anyone else, far as I know.

"I don't know if she tried to fetch the wish and failed, or if she didn't have the heart to try, but when Cristabel left that room, Penny's sister was as sick as ever. She died a few days later."

I peered over Gram's shoulder, through the open door, to the wall where Ma's picture hung. She was so goodly and beautiful. You could tell she was the sort of person who'd give a neighbor her last egg.

"Things weren't ever easy in the Walton house," Gram

added. "But after Loreen passed . . . I imagine Penny's life seemed unbearable. Seemingly, all because her good friend Cristabel—who fetched wishes for complete strangers—somehow let Loreen die. Betrayed, is how Penny must have felt. So, you might see why she's so angry. Course that don't make it right, her interferin' with that job for Dale."

I could only nod.

"You got to understand," she said. "I kept this from you for your own good. There weren't nothing you could do about it, for good or for ill, as a child."

But the truth was, I didn't *really* understand why she'd kept it from me. It was a sad story, but nothing I couldn't bear.

"Do you see now?" Gram called me back from my thoughts. "Do you see why we got to keep things quiet? With the problems we got, the last thing we want is more trouble. More folks . . . needing things we might not be able to give."

She set her head in her hands and let out a lone sob.

Something still wasn't adding up. Why was Gram so upset? Why had she been so secretive about a dying girl and a sorrowing family? I wanted to ask, but Gram's pain called me to her. I went to set an arm around her shoulder.

"It's all right, Gram." I soothed her as best I could.

I can't say I was glad she'd kept things from me for so long, but the truth was, even if I *had* known about all this business beforehand, I wouldn't have acted any different. I couldn't regret helping folks. To turn aside from another person's suffering—that was downright unneighborly!

But I had heard Gram's sorrow, too. From now on, I'd be more careful. Stir the pot more gentle-like. I'd lay the lemons on the table and show Sass I knew how to make lemonade. Maybe, someday, I'd even nudge my way toward Penny Walton's good side.

"What's in your head, Gen Sweet? I can see the wheels a-turning." Her voice was thick with woe.

"Don't worry, Gram," I told her. "All shall be well."

And I believed it. I really did. With all of my heart.

If only I knew why Ma hadn't been able to save Loreen Walton.

13

A WISH FETCHER'S BURDEN

TWO DAYS LATER, THE PRESS ARRIVED.

It began before dawn with a knock on the door.

Half dreaming and figuring it was Missus Fuller come to have tea with Gram, I went to the door in a hand-me-down robe that hung open to reveal my pink *Prom Queen*–themed pajamas. My hair was unbrushed, as were my teeth. I'm sure I had a heap of sleep in the corners of my eyes.

"Genuine Sweet?" asked the voice of a woman far too alert, given the time of day. She also pronounced my name wrong.

I couldn't actually see the woman. The pre-dawn dark, combined with a mess of blinding TV lights, prevented that.

"It's Gen-u-wine, but . . . yeah?" I shielded my eyes.

"Kathleen Kroeger, *Ardenville in the Morning*." By the time I understood that this had been her way of introducing herself, she'd turned her back on me. "Are we rolling? Darnell?

Can you get us rolling?" A red light blinked. Suddenly, and if it was possible, Miz Kroeger was even perkier. "This morning I'm in Sass, Georgia, talking to Genuine Sweet, who claims that she's a fourth-generation wish granter—"

"Fetcher," I corrected. "Uh—"

"—who's made the dreams of hungry people around the world come true. Genuine, sources tell me that the recent successes of groups like WorldFeeders and Les Estomacs Heureuses are due entirely to you—"

"I wouldn't say 'entirely'—"

"—and your magical wish muffins."

"Biscuits."

"Can you tell us more about this gift of yours?" She thrust a microphone at me.

Oh no, oh no, oh no! If Gram was tore up about an online profile, she'd fall to pieces over a TV interview!

"There's really not much to say," I assured her. "Not much to it at all, really. Sorry to have wasted your time. Have a nice day."

I tried to shut the door.

Miz Kroeger reached out an arm and flung the door back. She didn't look as perky as she had a minute ago.

"So you claim these muffins *don't* contain actual magic?" Miz Kroeger demanded.

"No! I mean, yes, they do, but—"

Just then, Jura came tearing up.

"Genuine! Wish to End Hunger — we've gone viral!" she gasped.

"Viral?" Was someone sick?

"Our hunger campaign," she explained. "It got picked up in the blogosphere!" She handed me an armful of printed pages:

HUNGER RATES PLUMMET ACROSS AFRICA (*BigApple News.com*)

FEWER ASIAN KIDS GO TO BED HUNGRY THIS WEEK (*NewzFerst.com*)

ANTI-HUNGER GROUPS FLOODED WITH DONATIONS AND VOLUNTEERS (*ArdenvilleNews.com*)

"Hello-o?" Miz Kroeger let her microphone fall. "I canceled an interview with the deputy mayor's secretary to be here. The deputy mayor's *secretary.* You are going to cough up the story, right?"

"Definitely. Absolutely," replied Jura. "Give us just one second."

Jura and I stepped out onto the porch, both of us grinning awkwardly at what appeared to be a news crew. Meanwhile, Pa was snoring on his apple crate and I'd just realized I was still in my pajamas. My dignity hung by a thread.

"Did you know about this?" I asked my friend.

"They only *just* called me. I know it's early for an interview, but it seemed like such a great opportunity to —"

"*You* told them to come on? Jura!" I whisper-hollered. "I cannot do this interview. You have got to send her away!"

Jura's chin jerked back. "What do you mean?"

"I mean what I said. No interview. People in Sass like things quiet. TV interviews aren't quiet!"

"Genuine!" She gripped my sleeve. "Your power can change things! You deserve to be heard!"

"I don't want to be heard." I glanced at Gram's shut door. Was she really sleeping through all this ruckus? "I want to be left alone."

"You can't be serious!"

"All right, kiddies." Miz Kroeger ambled up. "I want an interview about the wacky world of Genuine Sweet, wish granter, right now —"

"No!" I told her.

"Unless you *can't* grant wishes, in which case I'll assume this has all been a hoax, and I'll run a story about Genuine Sweet, international wish-granting fraud."

There it was. The straw that broke the donkey's back. Rather than let Miz Kroeger ruin my family name on TV, I gave her the interview.

Miz Kroeger picked up her microphone. "Are we rolling, Darnell?" She wiggled her shoulders and started back in with her perky voice. "Genuine Sweet claims to be a fourth-generation wish granter—"

"Fetcher," I corrected again.

"—and people are starting to believe her. Genuine's magical wish muffins are making news in the worldwide hunger-relief community, where some say that, after eating Genuine's wish muffins, their organizations experienced an increase in donations and volunteerism, as well as a decrease in governmental red tape. One organization even claims that one of these Sass-baked pastries ended a weeklong sandstorm, enabling relief trucks to reach remote villages in South Ethengar.

"You must feel very proud, Genuine!"

That seemed to be my cue. "I, uh, wouldn't say proud, precisely—"

"And eager to prove yourself!"

"No, uh, not really—"

"So, how about it, Genuine? What if we picked a random person off the street and asked them to make a wish? Could you grant it—on live TV?" She made a show of looking left and right. "Ah! Here's someone now! Hi! Hello? Could you help us?"

I'll be danged if she didn't drag one of the Fort brothers out of the shadows! He was dressed in his finest suit and wore a FEELIN' SASS-Y! baseball cap on his head.

"Happy to." Billy Fort beamed.

151

"Young Genuine here is a 'wish granter.'" Miss Kroeger made quote marks in the air. "And we were wondering if you'd like to make a wish for Genuine to grant, live on *Ardenville in the Morning!*"

Billy, who never was the sharpest tack, had his answer ready so fast I was sure he'd been coached. "Sure I would! I wish—"

"Hey! Hold up!" I threw myself between Billy and the camera. "I ain't fetching no wish on TV!"

"Excuse me?" Miz Kroeger demanded.

"I said I'd let you interview me, and I am, but wish fetching is private and solemn and . . . special! It is not made for entertaining folks while they drink their morning coffee!" I felt my face heat up with real anger. "And besides, people are hungry! Folks need medicine and whatnot! This isn't a game, you know!"

Miz Kroeger bumped Billy Fort aside and spoke into the camera, "Pointed words from a young activist. When *will* we stop treating hunger like a game?"

There were other questions, and I must have given other answers, but they were little more than a blur and a muddle. Then, just as quickly as she'd come, Kathleen Kroeger was "signing off, Blake."

I sighed in relief as she drove away, but I couldn't help getting mad all over again when I saw that her gas-guzzler had torn up our yard with its big chunky tires.

From atop his apple crate, Pa gave a raucous snort of a snore. I put my head in my hands and moaned.

When I looked up again, Darnell, Miz Kroeger's camera-man, was standing in front of me.

"Sorry about . . ." He jutted his chin in the newswoman's direction.

"She always like that?" I asked him.

"Always." He hefted a camera bag over his shoulder. "And always this early."

Just then, Jura reappeared. "You handled Kroeger really well! That was great righteous rage!" She shuffled some papers, dropping a few on the ground. As she picked them up, she said, "Now, uh, don't panic, now, Genuine, but with the whole 'going viral' thing, wish requests have kind of . . . tripled."

"What!"

She set a stack of Cornucopio messages in my arms. "Try not to worry. Travis and I are taking today's batch of biscuits to the post office as soon as they open. Did you know he helps his mom with her business? He's really good at this stuff! Anyway, once we get to school, the three of us can put our heads together and try to figure out . . . some-thing."

I nodded dumbly. Jura dashed off.

It took me a second to realize the cameraman was still standing there.

"I hate to bother you, but is there a good breakfast place in town?" he asked. "The crew is starving."

I told him there was, and if he could wait while I got dressed, I'd walk him down to Ham's. He said he'd be glad to.

I went back in to tell Gram I was leaving early.

Her door was still closed.

"How did Miz Kroeger find out about me, anyway?" I asked Darnell as I pushed open the door to Ham's.

Overhead, the bell jangled, though I don't know how anyone could have heard it over the din of conversation and silverware on plates. The place was packed.

"She gets her leads from all over," Darnell replied loudly. "Social media. Anonymous tips. She's not picky."

There didn't seem to be much to say to that, so I showed Darnell to the counter, wished him a pleasant day, and headed into the kitchen to order up a breakfast burrito. Both me and Jura had a few free meals coming our way — Ham's way of thanking us for arranging a barter that finally got him his new freezer.

"It'll be a few minutes," Ham told me. "We've been bustin' at the seams all morning. Who's that you brung in?" He nodded his head toward Darnell.

"Cameraman," I replied, taking a cup of milk the waitress handed me. "Thanks, Sue."

"Cameraman for what?" Ham slung a little hash with his spatula.

"*Ardenville News in the Morning*, I think," I replied.

"This about your wish fetching?"

I made a face. "How'd you guess?"

"A thing like that just draws attention," Ham said. "No fault of yours. The town spotlight even turned on your mama, back when."

"Yeah. I heard."

Ham's eyebrows rose. "So, your granny finally told you about Loreen Walton, did she?"

All at once, I had a thought.

"Ham, *you* don't know what happened there, do you? With Loreen's dying in spite of Penny's wish?"

Ham frowned. He looked over at Inez, the short-order cook. "Could you take over for a few?"

"Sure." Inez reached for a spatula and gave it a fancy flip.

"Come talk to me, Genuine, while your burrito's grilling." He hitched a thumb toward the back door.

Outside, Ham offered me an upturned bucket to sit on, then dragged over another one for himself.

Hunkering down, he began, "I believe you know your mama and I were good friends."

"Yes, sir."

Ham wiped his sweaty brow with a rag. "You resemble

Crista in a lot of ways. You take things hard to heart, just like she did. You try to fix stuff, even when it wasn't you who broke it. Just plain old good-spirited girls, both of you."

He looked at the pavement and sighed. I got the feeling he was deciding how much he should say.

"You *do* know what happened!" I realized.

He nodded. "I'm probably the only one she did tell."

"Ham, you gotta tell me."

"There ain't much to it, really." He shrugged. "Crista goes into Loreen's sickroom, tells the girl, *I'm here because Penny asked me to help you.*

"*Help me how?* says Loreen. And Crista tells her how she could fetch a wish to take the sickness away. Loreen listens real careful and gets quiet for a long time. Finally, she says, *Thank you kindly, but I'd rather walk the path the Maker laid out for me.*

"Crista was bowled over! A girl, not even twenty years old, dying, what didn't want to be saved? But they talked for a while, and Loreen explained how she'd rather go with her head held high, instead of grubbing and filching for time that wasn't hers. So what was Crista gonna do? Force a wish on the girl? Course not."

I saw it clear as crystal. Ma had been torn between Penny's good-hearted wish and Loreen Walton's *final* wish to finish things in the manner that felt right for her.

"So, she never even tried to fetch it." Distressing as it would be, I couldn't help thinking I would have made the same choice.

"Nope," Ham said. "Though she couldn't tell Penny that. I mean, how would it sound? *Hey, Penny, your sister would rather die than stay here with you?*"

When my jaw dropped, Ham added, "I don't mean to be that way. It's just, there weren't no good way for Crista to tell Penny the truth. Not when Penny was already so heartbroken."

"So Ma let the Waltons think it was her own failing that Loreen died."

Ham sighed. "And Penny never forgave her."

I peered down at my shoes. They were dirty to the tops of the soles.

"You all right?" Ham asked.

"I'm fine," I told him. "It's just, Gram made such a big to-do of keeping this from me." I gave a little half-laugh. "I don't suppose you know why?"

"That I can't tell you." Ham patted my shoulder. Jutting his chin toward the diner door, he added, "I gotta get back in there."

"Sure."

"Genuine?"

"Hmm?"

He locked his eyes on mine. "Of all the family shines in Sass, wish fetching is surely one of the most burdensome." He tapped his chest. "Taxing on the heart, is what I guess I'm trying to say. Go easy on yourself. All right?"

I didn't know precisely what he was getting at, but I could tell he meant it kindly. "Yeah. Thanks. All right."

14

WAITING LIST

I WAS LATE GETTING TO CLASS AND, ON TOP OF IT, HAD to ask Mister Strickland for more time on my math homework, seeing as how I hadn't cracked a book in nearly a week. He only shook his head and told me to see him after the bell. Truth to tell, it was hard to get too worked up about it. In the quagmire of biscuit baking and family secrets, Mister Strickland's anger hardly vexed me at all.

Even so, my thoughts were churning. A late assignment didn't count for much one way or the other, but what *did* matter, really? Feeding the hungry? Pleasing Gram? Helping my neighbors? *All* those things were important.

But what about me? Could I just keep on doing and doing until I dropped? Another twenty Cornucopio requests had come in that morning. When all of this was done — if it ever *was* done — would there be anything left of me?

When the lunch bell rang, I meandered up to Mister Strickland's desk.

"You wanted to see me, sir," I reminded him.

He nodded. "Miss Carver explained about your biscuit-baking backlog, and I've thought up a makeup assignment for you. It may solve some of your troubles."

I gave a sad little groan, thinking that the last thing I needed was one *more* assignment I didn't have time for. But suddenly, there was Mister Strickland, explaining about something called a waiting list. My assignment? To create a *prioritized* waiting list to manage all the incoming wish requests. I'd sift out the folks who were in dire straits and help them first. Then would come the people whose need was less urgent. Last on the list would be the folks who didn't have *needs* so much as *wants*. I nearly hugged Mister Strickland when I realized his idea meant I could actually get a full night's sleep that evening—and every evening from then on!

Jura was waiting for me out in the hall.

"Everything okay?" she asked.

"Better than okay, maybe," I replied, then told her about the waiting-list assignment.

Jura slapped her palm to her brow. "Triage! Of course! Why didn't I think of that?"

"Maybe we should put him on the board of directors," I joked.

"Oh. I almost forgot." Jura reached into her purse. "Travis gave me this to give you."

She handed me a paper folded in the shape of a bowling pin. I couldn't help but laugh. Unfolded, the page read, *We eat around six. The oven's waiting for you. Genuinely looking forward to it.*

Between the Tromps' bigger stove and the new waiting list — which I'd get done before day's end, even if it meant skipping lunch — I really might be in bed by ten!

"Travis saves the day," I said to myself.

"Huh?" Jura asked. Something near Sonny, over by his locker, had caught her eye.

"Nothing." I put the note in my pocket, a confidential little smile on my lips.

I might have kept on smiling, too, had Sonny Wentz not sauntered over to ask Jura if he could walk her home after school.

"Oh, and you, too, Genuine," he added.

15

BLOSSOMS IN WINTER

D ISAPPEARED DADDY OR NO, IT WAS HARD TO imagine anyone being surly for long living in the Tromp house. I'd passed by it, of course, but seeing as how the place was surrounded by a big fence, and considering that I'd never felt moved to go inside before, I was more than a little surprised to find out they'd been concealing paradise behind their gate.

I knew, like everyone else did, that Miz Tromp had some kind of herb-growing business making medicine teas and oils that you smear on your skin, but somehow I had never considered the size of the operation. Their tiny house, a wooden cabin hand-painted with a thousand brightly colored birds, was surrounded by five acres — easy — of plants in boxes and plants in bowls, of blossoming vines climbing trellises shaped like horns and hearts and hoops. Tomato bushes bowed with their red fruit, while rows of purple-faced lettuces and collard greens burst skyward, as if they were grateful somehow. And beyond that, there was a whole orchard of apple and peach trees, plus great swaths of a tall-stalked plant I thought might have been bamboo. In the middle of it all, a small pond with a fountain spouted water from a statue of a girl holding a watering can.

I just stood there for a while listening to the falling water and the ringing of the wind chimes that hung from the eaves of the house. After a time, though, some movement caught my eye, and there was Travis squatting in a clump of basil, collecting leaves.

"That's not for your nasty cigarettes, is it?" I asked.

He jumped. "Oh! Genuine! Naw, just helpin' out my ma." Now he smiled. "You look pretty tonight."

"Friends don't tell friends they look pretty," I schooled him.

"You girls talk about who's pretty all the time!" he countered.

The other girls did, it was true. No one ever said it of me, though. Suddenly I was very sure I didn't want to own up to that.

"Well, then, you look pretty, too, Travis."

He led me through the garden, glancing over his shoulder every two or so paces. "Let me hold those for you," he said, taking my starlight-harvesting buckets.

Off to one side, a metal contraption caught my attention.

It was something like a staircase, about eight feet high, with four wooden crates fixed to the top of it and a bunch of pulleyed ropes dangling down.

"What's that?" I asked.

"What?" Travis looked to see where I was pointing. "Oh, that's the harvester. Ma's picky about bruises on her custard apples. For a long time, we was having to climb up, bring down what few apples we could carry in our arms, then climb back up again. Which was fine before business got good, but now we're too busy for it. So I made that for her. She can climb up one time and set the fruit in the crates real gentle. Then, with those ropes, we can lower the boxes down and land 'em soft." He shrugged. "Looks funny, but it works good."

The perfect tool for the job, was how it seemed to me. With Travis's smarts and his handyman know-how, it was hard to imagine how even the stars could do better.

Travis walked me to the cabin door, set his hand on the door handle, and said, "Sorry if the place smells funny. It's Ma's herbal fixin's."

But the house didn't smell funny. It smelled *miraculous* — sweet like chocolate and spicy-clean like a summer day at the river. There was the impossible, otherworldly smell of newborn babies and the scent of good grandmas leaning over your shoulder while you're puzzling out your homework. I even caught a whiff of snow and spring rain.

"How does she do it?" I asked, whispering with the sheer wonder of it.

"Do what?" Travis asked.

I was still trying to find the words when Miz Tromp appeared.

"Genuine! Welcome!" She held a bunch of celery in one hand. "You got that basil, Travis? Toss it in the pot, will you?"

"Anything I can do to help?" I asked, following them both into the kitchen.

Every burner on the stove was taken up by a pot billowing clouds of steam into the air. The counters were full, too, with bowls and cutting boards and vegetables in every hue I could name. My stomach rumbled.

"She could decorate the cake, Ma," Travis said.

"Sure," said Miz Tromp. "Cake's on the top shelf, orchids on the bottom."

Travis went to the fridge and came out with a white cake so perfect it made me croon. With its rounded edges and fluffy icing, it couldn't possibly be anything other than store-bought. Real food just didn't look like that!

Travis set the cake on a table and went back to the fridge. "It was gonna be a wedding cake, but the bride chickened out," he explained.

"Travis, be nice," said his ma. "It is true, though. It was going to be a wedding cake. I do like to cook for guests, Genuine, but I normally don't go to *that* much trouble."

"You made this?" I asked.

"I did," she said. "If you're interested, I can teach you how someday. Meantime, though, pretty it up for us, will you?"

Travis set a box at the edge of the table and pulled off the lid. It was filled with flowers.

"You decorate a cake with flowers?" I asked, not exactly sure what I thought of that.

"You can eat 'em, see?" Travis took one and ate it.

When he offered me one, his ma piped up, "Those are for the cake!"

I took the yellow flower from Travis and traced the dashed stripe that ran the length of one of its petals. "Really? Right on the icing?"

He nodded encouragingly.

Carefully, I set the flower at the very center of the cake. It made me smile — though it took me some time to figure out why. I'll tell you now, but I don't expect you'll understand it.

You know how things stop growing in winter and all the trees are bare? That flower on that white-iced cake made me wonder, for just a second, what it would be like to live in a world where flowers could blossom in winter, where in spite of freezing weather, the alive things kept on growing, as if to say, "You can't stop me!"

Sounds silly, I know.

Travis handed me the flowers one at a time until I'd used up the whole box.

Miz Tromp looked over her shoulder while she stirred something on the stove. "Very nice. Maybe I should hire you."

"Genuine's already got a job, Ma. She's a wish fetcher," Travis said.

"Mm. So she does. I want to talk about that over dinner, Genuine. Whatever happened to my wish?" She said it with a smile, though, so I knew she remembered I'd told her to be patient.

In all my born days, I'd never had such a supper! Travis heaped up so much spaghetti onto my plate, there was barely enough room for fancified greens and bread with olive paste — which may sound peculiar but nearly brought tears of joy to my eyes. When he got to serving the meatballs, one actually rolled off my mountain of food. Thankfully, I caught it with my napkin before it hit the floor.

"Uh, maybe I'll just take this one to Gram," I said and set it aside.

Full up and feelin' fine, Travis and I did the dishes while Miz Tromp packaged the leftovers — including a whole *bag* of goodies for me to take home. Then I quick ran out to whistle down some starlight, and Travis and I got to baking.

We were pulling our first triple-sized batch of biscuits from the oven when there came a knock at the door.

"I'll get it," Miz Tromp said. "I wonder if it's the Teagues, changed their mind about the wedding cake."

"Tell 'em they're too late!" Travis called. He'd managed two slices, even after his own outsized dinner.

We heard some mumbling in the hall, and then Miz Tromp reappeared with Edie Walton, Penny's daughter, and a man I'd never seen before.

"Some folks to see you, Genuine," Travis's ma told me.

"Edie! What are you doing here?" With the upscuddle between her ma and me, I was fairly certain it was nothing good.

Edie, who'd graduated from Sass Public only last June, was the prettiest girl in town. She had long blond hair and dimpled cheeks and a smile so sweet folks said she could charm the moon from the sky.

But she wasn't smiling now.

"I need to talk to you, Genuine," was all she said.

"Your grandma told us we might find you here," the man said to me. Giving the Tromps a regretful smile, he added, "Sorry to interrupt your evening."

"We 'preciate the apology, but who *are* you?" Travis asked, stepping between the man and me.

"My name's Tom Holt." He offered Travis his hand. Travis shook, wary but civil.

"Please, both of you, sit down," Miz Tromp said. "You, too, Genuine. Can we get y'all something to drink?"

The man said he'd be glad for some water, but Edie only shook her head and sat. With nothing else to do, I took a seat, watching helplessly as Miz Tromp pulled Travis with her into the kitchen.

"What's all this about, Edie?" I asked.

Edie opened her mouth, tried to say something, and started to cry. I rushed into the kitchen, grabbed a handful of Miz Tromp's fancy paper napkins, and offered them to her.

When she finally collected herself, Edie said, "My mother didn't want me to talk to you, but Tom—Tom saw you on the news and he said, *Aren't you neighbors? What could it hurt?* And so here we are, you know?"

"Sure." I nodded encouragingly. "That makes sense." Though, I confess, I was hoping it would make more sense soon.

Tom spoke up. "I work at the Ardenville Cancer Center. I'm a nurse there."

Edie slapped her fistful of tear-damp napkins on the table. "My mom is sick, Genuine! Really, really sick!"

"I—I'm sorry, Edie," I said, and I meant it.

"We thought she was going to get better, but all at once, it struck her worse than ever. The pain—it hurts her so bad she *cries*, Genuine!"

I tried to imagine a pain that terrible. Even when I had broken my arm — and that smarted something terrible — I shouted, but I never bawled.

Miz Tromp drifted in and set a glass of water before Tom. Travis, I saw, lingered within hearing, leaning just inside the kitchen door frame.

"We — Tom and me — we were hoping you might come and talk to her." Edie sniffed. "See if you can wage some kind of peace between you two, so maybe she'd accept one of your wishes." She leaned forward. "A wish *would* fix her, right?"

"Truly? I don't know, Edie," I told her. "Maybe. I've never tried to fix a sickness before."

"But you could try, couldn't you?" Edie asked.

I dropped my chin to my chest. *Could I?*

Part of me wanted to. After all, I knew what it was like to be bad off and alone, wishing like mad for some prospect of help.

"Even if you could just help the pain some," Edie pleaded. "She's so tired with it. She can't even sleep!"

"Late last night," Tom said, "I went in to check on Penny. She wasn't in her bed. Finally, I found her in another room, sitting with another patient — a girl who was sick from her treatments. Penny was hollow-eyed and trembling with her own pain, but there she was stroking this girl's back, whispering, *You can do this, sugar. You're a fighter.* She stayed there till the girl nodded off." Tom pressed his lips together.

"Penny made me swear I wouldn't sneak in one of my alternative medicine 'crazies' for her. But seeing her caring for that girl . . . Please try, Genuine. Talk to Penny. And if she's willing, use whatever tools you have—"

I looked at Edie. Her lip trembled, but besides that, she'd gone utterly still.

The smell of fresh-baked wish biscuits hung in the air.

"Can I say—nobody here is asking for a miracle." Tom seemed to think something over, then went on, "Well, maybe we are. Asking for one. But we're not *expecting* it. Some treatments work. Some don't. We know that. We accept it."

Edie nodded.

I searched out Miz Tromp, who stood in the corner, expression heavy, hand resting over her heart.

I said to her, "Can I talk to you for a minute?"

"Sure, honey." Her voice was soft.

She led me into the kitchen, past a worried-looking Travis, and out onto a little porch.

She'd barely closed the door behind us when I blurted, "I've got biscuits to bake and send!"

"I know," Miz Tromp replied. "You've been working hard."

"But I have to go. Don't I?" I asked. "I can't just leave Penny to suffer."

"I'm sure we can arrange—"

"But, then, what if I go to her, get Edie and Tom's hopes

all up, and Penny Walton turns me away? Or what if I can't do it at all? What if the stars don't have that kind of power?" My ma never did try her shine against Loreen Walton's sickness.

Miz Tromp stood with me, sturdy as an oak. "How can I help?"

I squinched up my face. "Could you come with me? Tonight? You and Travis both? And — also — could we drop off this first batch of biscuits at Jura's?" Was it too much to ask? I wasn't sure.

"I can be ready and out the door in under three minutes. Travis, too, I imagine. Isn't that so?" Miz Tromp knocked on a nearby window. I hadn't noticed it was open just a crack.

Travis's face appeared. He nodded. "Yes, ma'am. Jura's, then Ardenville."

I let out a sigh. "Thanks, y'all. To go off to a big city, not a friendly face around me — I don't know if I could do it!"

I was headed back inside when Miz Tromp said, "You are gonna give your grandma a call before we go, aren't you?"

"I'll have plenty of time to call from the road," I replied. "Tom surely has a cell phone he can lend me. If I can help Penny, I want to get on with it." Besides, I didn't want to give Gram the chance to forbid my going. After her secret-keeping about the Waltons, it was hard to know what she'd say.

Miz Tromp pursed her lips. "All right. Let's go."

16

WHAT COMES OF IT

OM, MIZ TROMP, TRAVIS, AND I PILED INTO TOM'S jeep. Edie took her own car; she'd be staying there with her mother till the end, one way or the other.

After we dropped off the biscuits at Jura's, it was nearly nine. The night air was thick with an unseasonable fog.

"Curious weather," Miz Tromp said. "Do you mind if I—?" She pointed at the radio.

Tom said that would be fine.

" . . . thirty percent chance of snow with temperatures dipping below freezing," the radio announcer said. "The Department of Transportation warns commuters to expect delays in the morning. Y'all be sure to drive careful."

"I'm glad we left when we did," Tom observed. "As it is, you three might need to stay overnight."

Stirring things up with Penny Walton *and* spending the whole night out? Gram would be beside herself!

I reckoned there was no point in putting it off now. "Tom, could I borrow your phone?"

He passed it to me gladly enough, but it took some help from Travis to figure out how the dang thing worked. Finally, though, I managed to dial home.

Gram answered on the eleventh ring.

"You all right, Gram?" I asked.

"Fine, fine. I was just nodding off," she replied. "What time is it?"

"It's late," I replied. "Listen. I need to tell you something, so try not to worry, all right?"

That caught her attention. "What's wrong? Are you hurt?"

"No, I'm fine. Everything's fine. It's just, um, I may be spending the night out."

"Out! Don't be silly! Out!" She laughed.

"I mean it, Gram. Something's come up." And then I told it to her. All of it. Edie's tears, Penny's sickness, the bad weather. "We might have to wait for the roads to thaw in the morning."

Gram was silent for a time.

You could have knocked me over with a feather when she finally said, "That's a good idea, Gen. You don't want to be traveling if the roads get icy."

"So—you're not mad?" I asked.

"Mad that my girl wants to help a neighbor? Mad that she can't let the suffering of another human soul pass her by? This is what the legacy's for, Gen. To help. To heal."

"B-but what about Loreen Walton, and Ma, and all that big to-do?" I protested. "What about small wishes and not offending folks?"

She sighed. "I was being silly."

"Gram, you're never silly!"

"Not true! Remember the year I decorated my Easter hat with caladium leaves because the lilies didn't bloom? That was downright silly, if you ask me."

That *had* been silly, but still— "Gram, what on earth has gotten into you? Just a few days ago, you were full of dire warnings and woeful tales!"

"Life is short, Gen. We got to do what good we can," was all she said.

"What about Penny's sickness?" I wanted to know. "Can the stars cure it?"

"Truthfully, Gen, I think they can do most anything," Gram replied. "But we have to let them. If Penny is willing, the stars'll answer. If she's not, well then, bless her heart and come on home."

I thought that over. "Some people think when it's your time to go, you ought to face your destiny with your head held high."

"So they do."

"How's a person to know which is which? When it's destiny and when to let the stars help out?"

"I reckon . . . there's a certain quiet knowing," she told me.

I looked over to see the glint of the streetlights reflected in Travis's eyes. I reached out and poked him in the knee. Not sure why. Maybe I wanted to check-see if he was really there.

"You're sure this is all right with you?" I asked Gram. "Will you be all right alone tonight?"

A little snappishly, she replied, "I'm a grown woman, ain't I?"

"Well . . . all right, then," I said. "See you around lunchtime, prob'ly."

"Come at your own gait, honey."

She hung up.

I held out the phone so Travis could shut it off.

"Everything fine?" he asked.

"Ye-ah." I gave an uneasy shrug. "Something just feels, I dunno, peculiar."

He glanced at Tom and Miz Tromp in the front of the jeep. "I know what you mean."

Somewhere about midway through the drive, I drifted off. When I woke, my head was on Travis's shoulder.

"Sorry," I said, peering through my unruly hair. "I didn't drool on you or anything, did I?"

He laughed. "No."

Up front, Miz Tromp rifled through her bag and came out with a water bottle for each of us. She handed one apiece to Travis and me, then murmured something to Tom. He smiled and took a bottle.

"Can I ask you something?" Travis asked me.

"Sure."

"How come you wanted me to come along tonight?"

"I couldn't very well invite your ma and leave you sitting at home," I teased.

"Naw. Really."

The truth was, it had just seemed like the natural thing to do. I was getting used to having Travis around. If I was gonna do something hard, he should be there.

"I reckon it's because"—I chewed on my lip—"you help me feel strong."

For a second, I thought he was going to try to hold my hand. He seemed to think better of it, though, and gently bumped me on the arm with his fist.

"Someday soon, I'm gonna ask you to wish-fetch me a new pair of pants," he said.

"Oh? Why's that?" I asked.

"'Cause you sure do make a fella feel like he's too big for his britches."

It was deep dark when Tom pulled his jeep into the Ardenville Cancer Center. The halls were quiet, and most of the patients were asleep. When I glimpsed Penny from the hallway, though, she sat wide awake, a mound of pillows and plush toys threatening to crowd her off her own bed. In the harsh hospital lights, her skin had a troubling, greenish cast. But it was still Penny, poised with a pen over one of those sudoku books, looking as angry as I'd ever seen her.

I was crossing her threshold when she swore, "Dang fool thing!" and threw the booklet across the room. It landed at my feet.

Penny saw me and snarled. "You!"

I picked up her game book and set it on a table. "Miz, uh—"

"W-who! Who told you?"

Edie stepped forward. "I brought her here, Mama."

Penny turned three shades of red, huffed twice, and swallowed down what was clearly an uprush of pain. "You brought her? Then you get rid of her!" She turned her face away.

I can't explain how, but right then, I had the clearest knowing that, as angry as Penny was, she was far angrier at herself than she was at either me or Edie.

"Miz Walton, please—" I tried.

"Get out!" she roared, then grunted—with the strain of shouting, I imagined. "I don't want to hear a word you have to say! Nurse!" She reached for her call button and mashed it with both thumbs. "Nurse!"

Tom stepped forward. "Penny, please, hear us out."

"Oh-ho! *You're* behind this! Mister Alternative Treatment!

Mister Fluff-My-Aura Man! Tell you what." She pointed a trembling finger. "You're fired. I want a new day nurse. Get your supervisor. We'll deal with this right now." Penny mashed the button again. "Nurse! A *real* nurse, please!"

A real nurse did come in, and a supervisor, and two other folks who I reckoned were some kind of orderlies.

Penny waved an arm. "I want these five, including my daughter and this—this nurse-of-false-hopes, out of my room! I told you people I didn't want any homeopathic pseudo-medicine anything, and I meant it!"

And there it was. Just as fast as we came, a security guard was muscling us out of Penny's room.

I was so stunned, I nearly let it happen.

But all at once, I saw a glint of silver through the window. The sky was blanketed with glowing clouds, as if a full moon hung beyond them. One lone star, just one, shone out.

A wisp of music, the faintest breath of it, whispered behind my ear. *All shall be well.*

"Waaaaait!" I bellowed.

Everybody—Penny, nurses, guard man, everyone— froze.

Now what?

I had one chance to get this right. I had to let Penny know that a wish might yet heal her.

"Please! Miz Walton!" I called. "My ma never tried to cure your sister. Loreen asked my ma to let her die!"

As soon as the words were out, I knew I'd yapped up heartily.

Penny turned small and smaller, folding in on herself. Sass's bold real estate lady was gone. The tiny woman who took her place was something like the husk of a person who'd wandered a desert for weeks but never found a watering hole. She didn't even seem angry anymore. Just . . . empty.

"That's enough from you," muttered the guard. "Let's go."

As he strode us down the hall and toward the lobby, Edie called back to her mama, but Penny didn't reply.

It was a fairly bleak scene, there in that lobby, with Edie sobbing her eyes out and Tom standing stiff as a statue while his supervisor fired him on the spot.

Here's what comes of it, I recalled Gram saying.

I could only nod and agree.

"I'm sorry," I said to no one in particular.

Then I walked out.

I didn't know where I was going, precisely, so I wandered for a time. Around the parking lot, into a pretty little garden that—if the cold kept coming—wouldn't make it through the night. On the far side of some roses, a staircase clung to the outside wall of the building. I squinted at it, following it up to a landing on the roof. Again, there shone a bit of silver, that same lonely star overhead.

I climbed the stairs like a sleepwalker, dazed. I wasn't

sure why I bothered. High up or down low, this would still be my biggest gaum-up yet.

I just had *to come,* I poked myself. *All for the sake of fixin' things that wasn't mine to fix. Edie's ma not speaking to her. Tom fired. Penny's spark snuffed out, maybe for good. Not to mention the starving folks whose biscuits didn't get made tonight!*

I glanced up and around, as if the night sky might hold some answer as to how things had gotten so strained. Of course, it didn't. And as for the rooftop, there were only a few flower pots and a bench for sitting. Ardenville was prettier than I imagined a city could be, though. From up high, its lights twinkled like low-to-earth stars.

The wind gusted then, so I couldn't be sure, but I thought I heard another scuffle down below. Tom's voice, maybe, and Travis's.

After a time, Travis called clearly from the parking lot, "Genuine? You around?"

I walked to the tippy edge of the roof and shouted down, "I'm here! You can just let the police know where to find me when they get here." For, surely, they were coming to arrest us all.

I was walking the roof's edge, imagining what it might be like to jump off and suddenly find I could fly, when a *chunk-thunk* sounded behind me. I turned to see a pair of doors opening. It was a freight elevator.

Edie stepped out, pushing Penny Walton along in a wheelchair.

They didn't say anything as they came my way, so I held my tongue and let the rush of cars on the highway fill the silence.

Edie wheeled Penny up to me, reached out and squeezed my hand, then left without a word.

"I don't like you, you know," was how Penny started us off.

"I was figurin' that." My feelings weren't hurt. Truth to tell, after yapping Pa's chances for that handyman job, Penny wasn't at the top of my list, neither.

She grunted, her face gone tight with pain. It was a while before she managed to go on, "Did you make that up, what you said about Loreen asking Cristabel to let her—?"

"I'm no liar, Miz Walton." I said it harshly, I'll admit. But looking at that poor shuck of a lady before me, I couldn't stay mad. "And it was told to me by the most truthful man I know. I believe him."

Penny let out a sigh.

"Darn it," she said.

For a time, Penny and I just looked out over Ardenville. A few snowflakes started to fall.

She said, "I used to love the snow."

"Used to?" I asked.

"These days, all I can think of is how gray it'll look after it's been sitting a while."

"Most days it melts while it's still white," I replied.

Penny nodded. "You're right. And yet I still keep thinking gray."

I tried to think of something kind to say, but the only thing that came was, "I imagine they give you lots of medicine here. And tests and whatnot."

Penny let out a strange sound, something between a sob and a laugh. "Tests!" she cried, and made the sound again, this time looking at the sky, shaking her head in disbelief.

"Tests and medicine!" Penny exclaimed. "You're right about that. I've had every test that ever was and then some! And you know what they say, Genuine Sweet? They say that I'm dying. That a cancer cell is more powerful than a person." Penny made a fist so tight it shook. "More powerful than all the prayers and wishes in the world. More powerful than all the saints and G—" She fell apart, bawling.

I finally understood why Penny had caused that big ruckus back in Sass. She was sick in her body, and heartbroken on top of it.

I reached out to pat her hair, but she didn't seem to like that, so I stopped.

"It wouldn't have been right, my ma forcing a wish your sister didn't want," I said.

She nodded. "I know."

"But you wish my ma had put a wish on Loreen, anyway?" I asked.

"No." Penny wiped her eyes. "I mean, in a way, I do. But not really. Do you know what it is? What I think it really is?"

I gave her an encouraging headshake.

"Loreen and I were more than sisters," she told me. "Of all my kin, she was the one who was kind to me. When I told her I wanted to sell houses someday, she didn't laugh or scoff even once. *I bet you'll be real good at that,* she said. And you know what? I am."

Penny was so proud right then, I couldn't help smiling.

"But then she was gone. Dead. And there I was, a young girl alone in a house full of—well. Suddenly, what I wanted more than anything was to follow where Loreen had gone. But a body fights against that. It conjures up reasons to live; any old reason will do. Oh, yes, I kept on, though it took a heartful of conjured hate to do it.

"But who could I hate? Loreen, for dying? The Big Man, for taking her? I wasn't near brave enough for that! So I got mad at your ma. And *real* mad at myself for hoping. I bound myself up in a ball of hate, bitter as poison. But a lifetime of rage has a price."

Penny shook her head in wonder. "It was me all along. I did it to myself! All those months and years, kindling and rekindling my ire. I was so, so angry." She licked her lips with a dry tongue. "I thought the hate was keeping me alive—most times I thought that, anyway. But the truth is, the rage was killing me.

"I . . . do believe that's how I ended up here, ill.

"And then comes little Genuine Sweet," she went on, "making people feel good, and saying wishes can come true! What good is a wish when it can't save a beloved sister? Tell me that!" She swallowed her pain again. "So there I was, a grown woman hating a child of twelve, stirring up strife." She looked my way. "I am sorry about that, Genuine."

I understood now. It was all right.

"I have got to stop this hating. I've got to let it go!" Penny grabbed my hand. "I need help."

That wasn't all she said. We talked for a time about Loreen, and about my own ma. It seemed Penny had known Ma nearly as well as Ham had. So the two of us sat on a rooftop in the middle of a strange city, her recalling two women I'd never known, and me bursting with giggles at hearing how Penny and Ma and Loreen had once worked up the courage to skip school and go down to the gorge. What with all their worrying that they'd be caught truant, they'd hardly had any fun, and even came back early. It wasn't until they got home that they found out it had been a teacher planning day. They hadn't been skipping at all!

Even when my ma had *tried* to break the rules, she couldn't quite manage it. I decided I liked that about her. Very much.

After a time, Penny ran out of stories.

"But it was nice to remember," she whispered.

A peaceful quiet fell between us.

I reached into my bag for a wish biscuit — it seemed like the time — and found I hadn't brought a single one with me! That beautiful batch I'd made at the Tromps' — I'd taken the whole thing to Jura's!

We'd come all that way! Penny had poured her heart out and asked for help! And now, here I was, about to tell her, *It's great that you're ready to change, and all, but you'll have to wait for me to run back to Sass and get you a biscuit?*

I was still floundering when music danced in my ear. The single star overhead shimmered silver. It was my shine calling to me, and I knew what to do.

"What's your wish, Miz Walton? Your exact wish?" I asked.

She dipped her chin while she thought. "I wish . . . to be happy. And to let go. Is that all right? Can I make two wishes?"

"It's all right by me," I replied. "But what about your cancer?"

She let out a soft sigh. "I don't know whether it's my time

or not. But I do know it's time for me to be the person Loreen would have wished me to be. That's what I want."

And so, like my ma before me, I respected a Walton woman's unconventional wish. Though I didn't have a cup to collect starlight, I whistled anyhow.

"Y'all come," I crooned.

In the way-up distance, the star blossomed with silver light, brighter and brighter, till it was the only thing I could see. Then, all at once, the starlight flowed, spilling down through the darkness, so radiant that Ardenville's electric glow turned faint as a flashlight at noon.

"It's beautiful!" Penny cried.

The quicksilver was just within reach when I realized it wasn't *pouring* down. Instead, it fell like silver snowflakes. Thousands. Millions of them.

"You ever catch snowflakes on your tongue, Miz Walton?" I asked.

She laughed. "Not for ages."

"I reckon it's time to start again." I grinned. "Aim for the silver ones!"

She craned her neck and gave it a try, but I could tell she wouldn't be able to do it alone. So I let off the brake on her wheelchair and rolled her toward a patch of silver flakes within her easy reach. She nabbed one, then another, shivering with delight as they landed on her tongue. A new breeze blew, though, carrying the starlight off a ways. I quick pushed Penny in that direction now. We had a hoot and a half, there on that rooftop, me rolling Penny all around, her alternately pointing and crying out, "Over there! There! Got one!"

By the time she'd tasted a good dozen or so, we were laughing so hard our eyes shone with their own silver water.

"Genuine, don't you want to try?" Penny asked, beaming.

"Naw. These are for you," I told her. Then I whispered Penny's wishes into the night.

And Penny kept on smiling, and we kept on laughing, and we chased snowflakes across the rooftop until the last of the starlight ones had fallen and we were chasing plain old snow for the fun of it.

"Oh, Genuine," sighed Penny.

"Yes, ma'am?"

"It's good, don't you think?"

I flared my nostrils and felt, for all the world, that my heart might burst. "Yes. I surely do."

Not long after, a heavy snow began to fall in earnest.

Tom was still fired; one too many times he'd tried to sneak a shaman, a faith healer — or a wish fetcher — into the cancer center, it seemed. But now that we were all good friends, Penny invited us five to spend the night in her room. There was a reclining chair for Tom and a little sofa where Miz Tromp could stretch out. Travis and I went to the nurses' station to ask for a heap of pillows so we could sleep on the floor, but they said that wasn't hygienic and brought us in a couple low cots instead.

They also brought us a tray of ice cream cups. Plus, Penny's room had cable TV—every channel! We scooped out chocolate, strawberry, and vanilla swirl with tiny wooden spoons as we watched a movie about a pod of dolphins who turned out to be space aliens. Travis and Penny and Edie and me laughed a lot. Tom and Miz Tromp seemed to spend a lot of the time whispering to one another, smiling and agreeing.

In time, folks started dozing off. All except for me and Travis, that is. Both of us were completely wore out and completely wide awake. We pushed our cots together so we could whisper-talk.

"Looks like Ma's wish come true." Travis nodded glumly in Miz Tromp's direction, then Tom's.

"Maybe. You're not happy for her?" I asked, less than pleased to see the oldy-moldy Travis rear his head.

"No. I am. I know she's been lonesome," he replied. "But it is worrying."

"What is?"

"What'll happen when he leaves, like Pa did? It took an

age for us to build our lives back up again. Ma workin' an outside job to keep her plant business open. Me, too little to do much but get in her way." He was truly anxious, I could tell.

"Things might work out different this time."

"Yeah." Scratching at a speck on his hospital blanket, he added, "You did good tonight."

"I ain't sure I did anything at all," I told him. "Penny seemed to do most of the hard stuff." Nudging him with an elbow, I joshed, "Bet you're wishin' tomorrow was a school day so we could have off for snow."

"Naw. Then I'd be sittin' at my desk doing sums, instead of spending the day with you." A touch flustered, he added, "You know. As friends."

I considered him, in his shaggy blackness. His dark jacket and Converse shoes with the boot chain sat on the floor beside his cot. Such a peculiar boy.

But for some reason, I found myself thinking of reaching out a fingertip to touch one of the snaps on the jacket.

This is Travis Tromp! I reminded myself. He could be angry and pushy and—I'll say it—a little chauvinistic, with all that "baby" stuff. He was as goofy as a snaggletoothed pup, too. But despite all of that . . .

Despite all of that—*now, don't you laugh*—

"I reckon you ought to kiss me now, Travis."

He didn't wait for me to ask a second time. His lips were

soft and warm, and I especially liked the way he interwove the fingers of his hand with mine. Suddenly, I was toasty all the way down to my toes.

He turned away, sort of bashful-like, but he was grinning. "My ma told me I might stand a better chance with a certain girl if I stopped operating under the influence of dumb."

"She's a wise woman, your ma," I said.

We fell asleep holding hands.

It was the cold that woke me up.

I wrapped myself in my blanket and looked blearily around. Penny and Edie snuggled together in the hospital bed. Miz Tromp and Tom and Travis all seemed fine. Nobody shivered, no one's covers were drawn up to their chin. And yet, there I was, my teeth chattering so hard I felt sure the sound would wake someone.

Pulling the blanket still tighter around me, I padded to the window just in time to see a meteor shoot across the sky, burning like a star.

Make a wish, I thought, recalling the old hem tale about wishing on shooting stars.

I wouldn't really do it, of course. It might break the wish fetcher's first rule. *But if I did wish, if I could wish, what would I choose?* My belly was full. I was surrounded by friends.

Truth was, other than some extra covers to stem my curious chill, I didn't want for a single thing.

17

DELAY

I WOKE TO THE SOUND OF TOM'S WHISPERING VOICE. "The pavement's a little icy. I say we wait until the sun's good and high."

"That's fine," Penny replied softly. "Y'all can stay and help me pack."

"Don't you want to give yourself a day or two, Mama?" Edie asked.

I cracked an eyelid and looked around. I was the only one still dozing. Miz Tromp, Tom, the Waltons, even Travis, all sat with breakfast plates on their laps.

"She's awake!" Penny smiled.

"Hey, y'all." I yawned. "What's up?"

"What's up," said Penny, "is that I'm leaving this place behind and heading for home!"

"Are you feeling better?" I asked.

"Much. Thank you." She really did look different. More peaceful-like.

A doctor hurried in. After a stern glance in Tom's direction, she began rattling off the reasons why Penny should not, must not—if she valued her health—even *consider* leaving the cancer center. Behind her, a nurse nodded her agreement.

"Thank you, Doctor," Penny said, once the doctor finished.

"So, you'll be staying, then," the doctor said.

"No. But you're painfully concerned about my welfare, and I appreciate that. So, I say again, thank you. And goodbye."

The doctor sputtered some, but the nurse was faster on her feet. "Let us take some blood and see how you're doing. If you still want to go after that, at least we can say we did all that we could."

Edie made a hopeful little noise.

"Ah. Liability. We real estate people know about that," Penny remarked. "All right. Take the blood. But get my release paperwork ready, 'cause I *am* leaving."

It was noontime before somebody came in to take Penny's blood, and nearly four hours rolled by while we waited on the results. Meantime, the six of us spent the afternoon playing scavenger hunt. The orderlies weren't exactly pleased to find us in their supply closet — twice — in search of a broom bristle and a garbage bag twist tie, but we were having a grand old time.

Every so often, I thought about calling Gram just to let her know I'd be late, but she'd already said to come at my own gait, plus she'd been a little testy that I'd been worried for her, so I reckoned I'd just see her when I saw her.

Finally, at three fifty-five, the doctor and nurse reappeared in Penny's doorway. They looked stricken, complete with pale skin and googly eyeballs.

"Bless Patsy!" Penny said. "You two look like you've seen a ghost!"

"May I sit down?" the doctor asked as she fell into a chair.

"What is it, Marta?" Tom asked the nurse. I recalled they'd been coworkers only the day before.

Nurse Marta held up a few sheets of paper in reply.

I got up, took the papers from her, and walked them over to Penny.

Penny skimmed the pages and started to laugh.

"What is it, Miz Walton?" I asked.

But she only laughed some more. Then she handed the paperwork to Edie. And while Edie didn't seem inclined to laugh, she did set her hand over her mouth, closed her eyes, and commenced making a sort of squeaking sound that got louder and louder until it turned into a yelping, "Aww-ha!"

I couldn't take it any longer. "One of y'all tell us! What does it say?"

It was the doctor who replied, "It says Penny is cured. No cancer. Not even a sign that there ever was a cancer."

"Ms. Walton is *well*," said the nurse.

"It — it was all a mistake?" I asked.

"It was *not* a mistake!" The doctor held up a manila folder and flung it open. "Here! Test results from one week ago! With her name right on them! Penny W-A-L-T-O-N! And she had cancer!"

"Maybe you read 'em wrong?" I suggested.

"I didn't read them wrong!" the doctor shouted. "Marta, draw some more blood. We're doing this again."

Penny swung her legs out from her bed, set her feet on the floor, and stood up. "No, we're not. You have your tests and your results, and I have a life to enjoy. I am going home."

Just so there was no room for an argument, Penny added, "If you'll just get those release papers. Now."

"It's impossible!" said the doctor as Nurse Marta shuffled her out the door.

While the others waited on the paperwork, Travis and I darted into the hall to retrieve some more ice cream cups. It was party time!

Juggling an armful of choco-van stripe, Travis said, "That was curious, wasn't it?"

"Which part?" I asked.

"Those test results. It's great, and I'm pleased Penny's not sick and all. But . . . one week there's a big old cancer and the next week there ain't? Don't it make you wonder? Maybe we don't understand things—afflictions and whatnot—as good as we think."

"Maybe. I can't really say." For, surely, I couldn't. Penny hadn't even wished her sickness away, precisely, but there she was, cancer-free. "All I know is, Miz Walton's well and I'm glad."

Travis thought that over and sealed it with a nod. "Kickin' cancer butt and takin' names."

I smiled. "So, everything's fine. Right?"

He looked sidelong at me. "Why wouldn't it be?"

"No reason," I replied. "No reason I can think of."

By the time we got Penny packed and settled into Edie's car, the weather was feeling a bit more seasonable—chilly, but not bitter. The afternoon sun had melted off the ice.

We were headed back to Sass.

18

HOLD UP

I WANT TO STOP THE STORY HERE FOR A MINUTE. You've been a real good listener, and I've made it pretty easy for you. There have been a few rough patches, but so far, things have tended toward the best good. That's gonna change here for a time, though, and I find myself wondering how you'll take it. Or . . . is this what you come for? The gritty stuff? The hard parts?

I've heard folks say that the ruts of our sorrow clear a way for the cool waters of joy to flow.

What do you make of that?

19

POWERLESS

Tom parked with his headlights pointed at my house so I could better see to unlock the door. The darkness was nearly complete. Not even a light on inside.

The ground was a little squishy underfoot, and despite the warmth of the heater in the jeep, I felt badly chilled. I was just itching to get inside and put on my dopey but warm *Prom Queen* pajamas and a pair of thick, dry socks. I couldn't wait to settle down on my own sofa and pull the covers up to my chin.

I turned the key in the lock and opened the door quietly, so as not to rouse Pa or wake Gram.

The house was cold, and too quiet.

I flicked the light switch. Nothing happened.

"Gram?" I called into the dark, feeling my way to her bedroom door.

It was open. Her bed was empty and unmade.

"Pa!" I shouted and started flicking every light switch I could find in the dark.

No light. No light and no power.

I raced out of the house and almost ran right into the grill of Tom's jeep.

"No one's here!" I cried. "Please! No one's here!" I shouted it desperately, as if I doubted they would help or care.

Tom and Travis and Miz Tromp were climbing out of the jeep, issuing their words of comfort as if they had any right to, as if they had any knowledge to pull from, when the flashing blue lights appeared. The swirling lamps turned the land into a haunted wood with strange, flickering shadows. They reached for me. They reached for Travis.

I was confused when Sheriff Thrasher appeared. Had I done something wrong? Was I being arrested after all?

"Genuine." The sheriff got down on one knee and looked at me eye to eye. "Your granny's in the hospital. If you'll come with me, I'll take you to her."

You'd think, in a moment like that, a person would have a million questions. *What happened? Is she all right?* But inside me, there was only an icy wall of silence. I got into the police car and noted, dreamlike, that Tom's jeep was following behind us.

★ ★ ★

The lights in the hospital were just as bewildering as the darkness at my house. How could anything be so glaringly bright? I shielded my eyes and followed the sheriff down the hall. My pa was passed out in a plastic chair beside one of the doors. The boozy smell of him wafted over me, another dreamy scrap of that night I'll always carry.

Sheriff Thrasher was about to open the door to Gram's room when Nurse Cussler rushed up and barred the way. She whispered to the sheriff. I know she meant for me not to hear.

"She died, Mike," was what the nurse said.

It wasn't true, of course. It just wasn't.

I darted between them, pushing past Nurse Cussler's stupid hearts-with-wings scrubs, and rushed into Gram's room.

Her mouth was open, her head tilted back just a little. The bright lights gave her a waxy look, and I saw clearly the strange green hue to her skin that I'd noticed a few weeks before. She wore one of those terrible, embarrassing hospital gowns. I wanted to take it off her and wrap her up in her warm terry-cloth robe. Where was her terry-cloth robe? I tore into the wardrobe, moved the table and chairs, opened every drawer I could find. The robe had to be there somewhere!

"Genuine." It was a man's voice, I think.

Someone touched me and I pushed them away.

"Genuine." They tried again.

"Go. Away." I said it in a voice that sounded strange and far off.

"Honey." This was a woman's voice.

A thumb ran over each of my cheeks, wiping away water I hadn't known I was shedding. I blinked. I shook my head. I found myself looking into Miz Tromp's dark eyes.

"Honey," she said again. "You're safe. You're okay." Her words made no sense to me. "You take as much time as you want here with your gram, and then you'll come home with us, all right?"

That much I understood. They wanted me to leave Gram. They wanted me to go someplace else, a place where Gram wasn't.

"No! No! I have to find her bathrobe!" I exclaimed. "I have to put it on her. She's sick. I have to take care of her!"

"She's not sick, honey," Miz Tromp said softly. "She's gone on to the next place."

I think it was those two words, *next place,* that broke over me like a storm.

She's dead. She's DEAD. She froze to death. The electric went out. The bill was overdue and you knew it. She froze to death, and you were off in Ardenville, looking after folks who weren't even yours to care for. You kissed that boy. She told you not to kiss him, and now she's dead. Your gram is dead and she died alone. She took ill in the dark and she surely must have called for you. Who else would she call for? She called and YOU WEREN'T THERE —

Even though my eyes were open, the world went black.

I fell for what seemed like hours. Days, even.

I remember waking up for a time and roaring angrily, "Where is my father?"

"We don't know," someone answered. "He left."

"Yeah," I said as the darkness took me again.

When I woke up, I felt like one big bruise. Not just in my body, but in my head, too. Heart and soul, everything ached. I couldn't remember why.

I opened my eyes.

I was resting on an orange sofa, an ugly one made of the sort of itchy fabric generally used for potato sacks. I could see a desk and some bookshelves, some books with titles that made me think I might be in a doctor's office. I looked around some more and saw diplomas on the wall. *Someone Someone, M.D.*

I was alone in there. And realizing I was alone was what made me remember.

Gram.

The doorknob turned, and the door made a little gasp as it opened. With a thrill, I realized it had to be Gram! All of this was a terrible dream, and when that door opened all the way, I'd wake up and find myself on the sofa at home. It would be morning, and Gram would be smiling down at me. *Time to wake up, Gen.*

But it wasn't Gram at the door, and I was already awake.

I knew a moment of hate, just then, at whoever dared to open that door, and whoever made that door and hung it on its hinges. I hated all the doors that had ever been and all the trees that had been torn down to make them. I hated—

"You're up," said Miz Tromp, who held a paper cup in her hand. "How are you feeling?" Gingerly, she set the cup on a table and shut the door behind her.

"Gram is dead, isn't she," I said. It wasn't really a question.

"Yes."

I nodded and asked, "What time is it?"

Travis's ma looked at her watch. "About nine thirty."

"In the morning?"

"Yes."

"Is it cold out?" I wanted to know.

"Not too bad."

"It was cold the night they brought her here," I told her.

"Yes. I know." She sat down on the sofa beside me.

"She died cold," I said.

Miz Tromp shook her head. "No. She died here, in the hospital. She was warm."

"The cold killed her, though." I knew it for certain.

"No, honey, she—"

The door opened again. It was Nurse Cussler with her stethoscope hanging out of one of her hearts-with-wings scrubs pockets.

"You're awake," she said.

I frowned. "We've established that, yes."

"Do you think you can eat something? I can get you—"

"I don't want anything." *Ever.* "Thank you."

And so they gave up on their nursing and mothering and got down to talking turkey. My pa had disappeared, and they didn't want to take me home to an empty house. How would I feel about staying at the Tromps' place until someone could locate my pa?

I shook my head sourly. "I just want to go home."

Several phone calls later, they'd arranged for Dilly Barker to come sit with me until Pa turned up. Besides being a kindly woman, Dilly was also our closest neighbor.

When Miz Tromp dropped me off, the electric was back on.

"The power . . . ?" I inquired.

"Tom rang every number the electric company had until he got someone on the phone who could turn your power back on." There was some pride in Miz Tromp's voice as she said it.

"Who paid for it? I'll have to pay them back."

"Oh, Genuine, don't worry—"

"Who?" I demanded.

"Travis and me," she answered.

"I'll pay you back."

"If you want to, honey, sure." She gave my arm a stroke.

I stepped aside, turned my back on her. "Does everybody know?"

"About what?" Miz Tromp asked.

I wasn't sure. About the way the help only came after it was too late, maybe.

"Never mind," I said.

Dilly sat on the sofa, knitting, taking all this in. In the quiet after I'd spoken, she said, "I sure am going to miss Starla."

For a second, I just looked at her, startled to hear someone say Gram's name out loud. Then I did the strangest thing. I went into Gram's room and got *her* knitting. I sat down on the sofa beside Dilly and started to *knit one, purl two*. I'd never knitted in my life, but I reckon I'd seen Gram doing it enough to recreate it on my own.

"Do you need anything, Genuine?" Miz Tromp asked.

I shook my head but didn't say anything.

"Then I'll leave you girls to your fancywork," she said, and left.

* * *

The pretty scarf Gram had been knitting now looked more like a long snake after a big meal. In short, I had ruined it. But I kept on knitting. I kept on until Dilly had to give me another skein of yarn. Then I kept on knitting until I fell asleep.

When I woke up, Pa's shoes were next to the sofa. His door was closed. There was a sandwich on a plate in front of me, and, beside me, Dilly Barker continued knitting away.

"Pa's here," I said. "You should go on home."

"Try to eat a little something," she said, but she didn't leave.

We knitted until suppertime. Then I followed Dilly into the kitchen and helped her reheat a casserole — one of about fifteen in the fridge.

"Some folks stopped by while you was asleep," she explained. "Nothing like a death to bring on a plague of casseroles."

Sunday blurred into Monday. Monday came and went.

Tuesday morning, Dilly Barker walked me to school — only because I'd told her I wanted to go — then headed back to her own house.

"I'll stop by later with some more yarn," she called out as she departed.

Jura was waiting for me on the front steps and wrapped me up in a hug so tight, I couldn't breathe.

"I only met your grandma that one time, but she was real nice," she said.

"She was nice," I agreed.

For a time, we were the only ones in the classroom. We sat at our desks, not saying anything at all, Jura rubbing my back with one hand. It felt good. And even though my heart hurt a lot, it was the kind of pain a friend really can help ease. Instead of thoughts of Gram by her lonesome, calling out for me, I thought—just a little—about Penny Walton and about Wish to End Hunger, too. Maybe it was time I dusted off my baking pan and got back to work . . .

Then Sonny Wentz walked in and hugged Jura like it was *her* gram who had died.

Only after that did he say, "Sorry about your granny."

He gave Jura a funny look, muttered, "Uh, I'll just sit over here, then," and reached for his book satchel—which had been leaning against the leg of *my* desk. I realized he was mildly confounded because *I was in his seat.* In the single day I'd been out of school, he'd taken my spot.

"Genuine—" Jura started.

"I—Are you with Sonny now?" I asked.

Jura cast Sonny a quick look.

"I'll just, uh—" he said, and walked off.

On one breath's worth of air, Jura blurted, "I figured it was okay. It *is* okay, isn't it? I mean, you only liked Sonny when you thought he liked you, right? But when you found out it wasn't him who'd asked you bowling, you didn't like him anymore, right?"

I was stunned silent. I don't know why. I *was* sorta with Travis now. I kissed him and liked him and everything.

I had to pry my clenched jaw apart to say, "Oh, sure. No. That's right. No."

"You look upset," Jura said.

Me, upset? Surely not! "Just surprised. Glad for you. Surprised and glad." It wasn't as if Sonny had given me any real sign that he liked me as anything more than a plain old, boring, ugly, ugly, ugly friend. Genuine *Beauty* Sweet. Ha.

"Do you swear this is okay?" she asked. "Do you *swear?*"

I conjured a smile. "Course."

I started to get up from my desk.

"You don't have to move." Jura set her hand on my arm. "Please stay."

"No, really. You two sit together. I'm not feeling much like company anyway."

Which is why, of course, at that exact moment, as I was moving my things to a desk in the back of the room, Travis appeared in the doorway.

He walked over and gave my wrist a squeeze. "Heard you was coming to school today."

"Here I am," I replied.

"I been worried about you, but my ma said I should let you alone for a while."

"That's fine."

I didn't know what to say to him. Suddenly, everything seemed so stupid. Could it really be that the world was still spinning? Didn't everyone realize how hollow all their comings and goings were?

"I brought two lunches. I thought you might have forgot yours," he said.

"I'm on free lunch." *Yup. I can cure cancer, but I still can't buy my own food.*

"Oh, right."

He stood there, looking at me like he expected something. *Just like everybody expects something. For themselves, of course. Not for me. Why worry about little Genuine? She's got her free lunch, don't she? What more does a poor Sweet need?*

"You should go to class now," I told him.

"Are you really sure you should be here today? I can—" He reached for my books.

"Please go," I said.

Sonny walked up, his chest all puffed out. "I believe she asked you to leave, Tromp."

"Sonny—" Jura darted over. Her wide eyes were the color of sweetgum honey. Even riled up, she was beautiful. No wonder Sonny wanted to be with her.

"Just go, Travis," I said, suddenly feeling so, so tired at the prospect that there might be a fight.

But Travis's attention was all on Sonny.

"Step off, Wentz," Travis snarled.

"Can't you even just leave her alone this one day? Don't you get it? You're not wanted." Sonny shoved Travis's shoulder.

"Sonny! Stop!" Jura said, gripping Sonny's sleeve.

"She doesn't even like you," Sonny continued. "Do you?" This last question was directed at me.

I looked up at Sonny, then at Travis. More than anything, I just wanted them to go away.

I think what I'd intended to say was, "I don't much like either of you right now."

I only got as far as "I don't—" when Sonny cut me off and said, "See!"

Travis's face went slack. Before I could make sense of the fact that I'd been misunderstood, he fled the room and slammed the door behind him.

The second bell rang. Immediately, the door opened again and Mister Strickland stood in the doorway.

"I'm sorry. I thought that was the bell. Why aren't you in your seats?" he demanded.

We had three hours till lunch. *Three hours* for Travis to steep good and dark, thinking I'd denied him.

I put my head down on my desk. I wanted so desperately to cry—over Gram, over Travis, over everything—but the tears just wouldn't come.

Finally, lunchtime arrived. Though I didn't feel like talking to anyone, I knew I should find Travis in the cafeteria and explain myself. But when I walked in and the smell of food hit me, I was suddenly so pukish I could barely stand.

"Are you okay?" Jura appeared and wrapped an arm around my shoulder.

Her closeness seemed to shut out the fresh air. I breathed those awful deep breaths you take when you're trying not to sick up.

"Can't —" I said, and raced out the door, down the hall, and into the bathroom.

Once I was in there alone, with my forehead on the cool blue tiles of the privy wall, the queasiness started to pass.

The bathroom door opened.

"Oh, good. I thought I saw you come in here."

I looked up. A girl strode in.

"Have you thought about my wish at all?" she demanded. "Because I'm sort of running out of time. If I don't —"

It took me a second to place her. *Ruby Hughes.* She'd asked me twice about wishing up some new tack for her horse. Some big hooray of a show coming up.

"Go away," I said.

"Look, Sweet, I know for a fact you granted Chastity Port's wish —"

"Go. Away."

With a goofy sort of roar, she ripped a handful of paper towels from the dispenser and threw them down on the floor. "You're not the first kid whose granny ever died, you know!"

She waited, as if she actually thought her foul words might have changed my mind! When it became plain they hadn't, she hissed, "Any fool can wish on a stupid star!" and stormed out.

After a sliver of a pause, I ran after her into the hall. Even though I was six inches shorter than she was and only two-thirds as wide, I grabbed her by the back of the shirt and spun her around.

"How about this, you cheese-eater?" I put my finger in her face. "How about you take your asinine horse show and stick it where the sun don't shine? Or! Or! Even better! Any fool can wish on a star, you say? How about you wish up your stupid tack for yourself? Oh, wait! You can't! Because you're useless, you prima donna, gonna-be-married-and-barefoot-this-time-next-year, and I'll tell you what, not a single person in this town is gonna give a care for your stupid horse or its tack! Or for you!"

I'm ashamed to admit, for about thirty seconds, I felt much better.

It was the thirty seconds after that that cast me into the breach. But even then, I didn't cry. It was more like a howl that somebody tore out of me, a sound so full of rage it wasn't even human. I slammed my open hand on one of the metal lockers and relished the racket as the sound rang through the hallway. I did it once more, bellowed, and took off at a run. I didn't stop until I was halfway down Main Street, at which point I realized there was nowhere I wanted to go, nothing I wanted to do, and no one I wanted to do it with.

Ham found me sitting on the curb outside his place. When he drug me to a booth in the back of the diner and set a cup of coffee afore me, part of me wondered if he was buttering me up for a wish.

Later, when he was closing shop — and it must've been much later, seeing as how it was getting dark out — he pressed a paper bag into my hands. I didn't thank him then, either, but he seemed to understand, and only patted me on the head and told me to "git on home, now."

I couldn't even rally myself to look him in the eye. I just got.

Outside my door, I found a pile of yarn, three casseroles, and a card addressed to *The Sweet Family*. I tore it open with a bitter chuckle.

The card had a seagull on it, flying over a blue sea at sunset. It read, *Deepest condolences* in one of those gold, curlicue scripts. Inside, Handyman Joe had written something sincere and sad. I tossed that card onto Pa's apple crate, which was currently unoccupied.

Just because it seemed like a waste to let food go bad, I walked the casseroles and Ham's paper bag to the fridge. It was strange to see how much grub had collected there since . . . that night. It wasn't so long ago that I'd sat looking at that empty refrigerator, my stomach rumbling, wishing for something more than thin broth and beans.

For a glimmer of a moment, I almost, almost felt grateful. Almost.

Out of the corner of my eye, I saw the electric bill poking from beneath the living room lamp. I stormed over, hefted the lamp, and snatched up the slip of paper.

> *Unfortunately, we do not accept payment in the form of goods and/or services. . . . Please note your current bill is three days overdue.*

I squeezed my eyelids together and crushed the letter in my hand.

It was time for a reckoning.

20

A RECKONING

THE CLEARING WAS EMPTY AND THE NIGHT WAS quiet. Squirrel Tail Creek carried pebbles and silt to a river that flowed to the Atlantic. Overhead, the stars went on with their beaming as they did night and day, regardless of who laughed or cried, lived or died.

"I want you to know something!" I shouted at the sky. "I remember Gram's story about the man from Fenn. How he felt all deprived when everyone but him got their wishes filled, and how it turned out badly when he started fetching wishes for himself. People cursing his name and whatnot. I remember every word of it!"

As you might expect, there was no reply.

"Let me tell *you* a story, stars! Once there was a girl. She was poor, but she was a wish fetcher. And she granted some wishes, and yeah, some people did her a good turn as a result. At least she wasn't hungry no more. She should have been pleased, right?"

Twinkle. Twinkle.

"But that's not the whole tale. Because this girl lost her ma, you see. And her pa's a drunk and a lout. And however much she fetched lost treasures or paired folk up with their soulmates or helped her best friend's ma get a good job in town, she couldn't bring her own ma back. Her father was still a stinking boozer. Sounds nice, don't it?

"But that's just the icing on the cake, stars! Because the real treat at the heart of all this wishing was that, for some blame-fool reason, the girl started to believe that everything was gonna be all right. *All shall be well*, you said! *All manner of thing shall be well!*

"*So* well that she never did turn up the money to pay the electric bill. *So* well that she went to Penny Walton's bedside instead of staying home where she belonged. So *well* that while she was gone, the electric went out and the snow began to fall and her most perfect gram lay there in the dark, alone, getting colder and colder — until she died!

"What do you think of *that* story, stars?"

My voice echoed in the empty night.

"So here's how the story ends. The girl says, *No more!* I'm not playing by your rules anymore!"

I held up my wish cup and whistled to the stars. "Y'all come, now. Y'all *come*."

My voice was bitter, but the stars didn't seem to mind. At last, and in their own way, they replied.

Even through the haze of my heartsickness, I had to admit it was as beautiful as ever, the quicksilver flow of starlight pouring down from way up on high. As the cup filled, I felt the impossible neither-cold-nor-hotness of it through the plastic against the skin of my hand. It defied every word of description I possessed, and all I could do was gape in wonder.

But if you think I was swayed by that splendor, you're wrong.

"Thank you kindly," I said.

I took that cup of starlight and drank it down.

I'll tell you straight up, there's no way I can make clear what it felt like, drinking that stuff. My knees nearly buckled; I know that much. A delicious chill rushed through me, from my tailbone up to the very top of my head. Around me, the edges of things—the trunks of the trees, the moonbeams, even the leaves and pine needles on the ground—turned vivid, their colors sharper, even through the dark. I breathed, and the air was me and I was it, and I could feel it fill up every part of me, every last cell.

But perhaps the real wonder was, in the face of all that rapture, I still managed to do the thing I'd come to do: balance the books.

"I wish for money!" I screamed into the night. "Lots of it!

And a better house and a sober pa. I wish a ma for every baby and for no one ever to go hungry. And most of all — you hear me, stars! — most of all, I wish for my gram back!"

I knew it the second the last words left my lips. I knew it before I held up the cup and tried to call down some more starlight — though I did do that, out of spite, maybe. I knew it as sure as I knew Pa would be drunk tomorrow and Gram would still be dead. I knew it.

The magic was gone.

Feeling little else but tired, I curled up on Gram's bed with her *Farmer's Almanac*. It talked about the stars and the seasons and the right days for planting all sorts of crops. Everything had its own special time.

I fell asleep thinking about how folks had been relying on star shine for centuries before Sass's Genuine Sweet came along.

When I woke up, Pa was snoring drunk — in front of the television, this time — wasting electricity paid for by the Tromps. I switched the thing off and told him, "Go to your own room," but he was well past hearing.

The miracle flour was still in the kitchen and as quick to replenish as ever. The stars hadn't taken that away. I made a batch of biscuits — plain, no starlight to them — and left a few on a plate by Pa's head. The rest I took with me to school. That way, I wouldn't have to go to the cafeteria for lunch, with its wish-hungry people and food smells and—

Travis, I suddenly recalled. I'd left him the whole night to sleep on the thing he'd thought I'd said. There, at least, was one thing that could be made right.

I took the back road to his house, past the Binset place, by way of Hound Dog Trail. When I got there, Miz Tromp was sitting on her bench swing, using her feet to push herself back and forth, back and forth.

"Howdy," I said.

She looked a little startled, as if I'd disturbed her from her thoughts. "Oh. Genuine. How are you, honey?"

I didn't have a civil answer to that, so I said, "I got biscuits. You want one?"

She shook her head forlornly.

"You all right?" I asked.

"I guess," was all she said for a time. "Travis's father called."

Hearing about another person's shakeup sometimes has a way of sweeping clear your own inner floor. I was instantly worried for Travis. He'd been troubled that Tom would leave Miz Tromp like his pa had. But instead, here was Travis's *actual* pa, come to stir things up again. What could it mean but trouble?

"What did he want? Is it bad? Is Travis all right?"

Her reply was too slow in coming. "Travis is all right, I think. His dad wants him to come visit."

"Oh. Well, that's not so—"

"And maybe to live with him. In California."

"California!" I exclaimed. "That's so far away! Surely Travis doesn't want to go!" After all, he was still so mad at his father. It was hard to imagine he'd even want to visit, much less stay with the man.

"It's a powerful thing," Miz Tromp mused, "to feel wanted. After all these months and years of being so heart-broken that his daddy didn't want him"—she paused, then repeated—"it's a powerful thing."

"So, Travis might r-really do it?" It wasn't possible! It wasn't right! We'd only just got to be . . . friends!

"He's flying out next week. For a visit. 'To start,' Travis said. So, yes. It seems he's thinking about it." Miz Tromp dropped her chin. "And to make matters more compli-cated"—she bit her lip—"Tom wants to open an alternative healing retreat. In Sass. And he says he loves me."

I stopped to replay her words in my head, just to be sure I'd understood her right. "Uh. That was quick."

"Foolish quick," she agreed. "Ridiculous quick. But here's the crazy thing. I like him, too. And I'd probably tell him, *Great! Come on!*, except that—how can I even *think* of falling in love, with all this other stuff going on? Travis moving to California? At least I'd have to go and make sure things are okay. I mean, I don't think Kip would get a wild hair and leave Travis on the roadside or anything, but *still*. We haven't seen Kip in *years*. I've at least got to make sure things—make sure *Travis* is all right!"

She threw up her hands. "Genuine! What if this is my wish coming to pass? What if it got divided up? A man for me: Tom. A daddy for Travis: Kip. What if, somehow, this is the best good?"

My head spun. I was angry and getting angrier. *All shall be well!* Yeah, this worriment looked mighty *well,* all right.

"So, I guess what it comes down to is this." Miz Tromp set her chin in her hands. "Do I owe you your vegetables now? Is Tom the wish you fetched for me? Is Kip the daddy for Travis? If only I knew for sure, things might seem . . . clearer." She set her eyes on me and waited for an answer.

I didn't know what to say.

Just then, Travis appeared at the door. He took one look at me, turned around, and walked away.

"Travis!" I was already on his heels when I called out, "Excuse me, Miz Tromp!"

I reached his bedroom door just in time for him to slam it in my face.

"Travis!"

I knocked. I pounded first with my fists and then, gently but sincerely, with my forehead. "Travis. Please open up."

He didn't even do me the courtesy of telling me to get gone.

"Travis," I spoke to the door, "I'm sorry. I'm sorry. What you think I said wasn't what I meant to say."

Not unlike the stars the night before, his only reply was silence.

"I wasn't saying I didn't like *you*. I was saying I didn't like either of you." I heard my words and knew they'd come out all wrong. Again. "Dog my cats, Travis, that's not what I meant. I meant . . . there you two were standing over me, getting ready to signify all manly, and I just didn't want any part of either of you, right then. Not because I don't like you, but just because I was so, oh, I don't know, far away. You understand that, don't you? Please understand that."

I waited to see if he'd say something. Finally, a sound came from his room, sort of a shushing, sliding sound.

A window opening! He was climbing out!

I raced out of the house, called out a quick goodbye to Miz Tromp, and caught Travis just as he was catching his balance against a trellis beside the house.

"Stop!" I shouted.

He stopped, but he turned his face away.

"Don't you know," I pleaded, "if you're moving away, we *got* to make our peace. I never liked anyone before, the way I like you—"

"What about Sonny?" he grumbled.

"Sonny's with Jura," I told him.

"That don't mean you don't like him."

"You're right," I conceded. "It doesn't. But I don't. Like him, I mean. I like you. I like *you*."

He still wouldn't look at me. "I got to go to school."

"Me, too. Want to walk together?"

He reached in through the window and pulled out his satchel. "Maybe you'd better take Earl Street."

In other words, no, he didn't want to walk together.

". . . All right, then. Maybe I'll see you at school," I said.

He cleared his throat and walked off.

I went back around the house—toward Earl Street—and heard Miz Tromp murmur as I passed by, "I wish there was a good solution to all this. There has to be one."

Halfway through third period, I got called out of class to talk to Missus Peeps, the school counselor. She was concerned about me, she said, and thought I might want to talk about losing my grandmother. I didn't, and I said so.

She nodded, all counselor-like. I thought that was the end of it.

I was about to get up to leave, when she said, "You've had a lot on your turkey platter lately. Not just your grandma, but the wish power and all the attention it's brought on you."

"That's all done now," I told her.

"Done, how?" Missus Peeps asked, frowning.

223

"I can't fetch wishes anymore."

"Can't? Or won't?" She said it like I'd offended her.

"Can't," I said. "Why? Did you want something?"

I'd meant it to be snarky, but her eyes actually lit up.

"Well, since you asked—" she began.

I got up from the chair and walked out.

After school, I headed to the library to delete the Cornucopio profile for good. Genuine Sweet's Wish to End Hunger was closing its doors.

As I marched down the sidewalk, chin jutting and arms pumping, it might have seemed like I couldn't get there fast enough. You might have wondered if I was pulling the plug out of spite. But it wasn't like I had a choice. I couldn't fetch wishes anymore. People might be starving, but just as they had with the troubles in my own hungry family, the stars only helped when they saw fit to.

Jura was waiting outside for me, as if she'd known I was coming.

"Hey," she said.

"Hey." I set my hands on the city hall/police department/historical society/library/extension office door handle.

She reached in front of me, gently blocking my way. "Are you mad at me?"

It would have been easy to say, *No, of course I'm not mad. It's just my gram dying. Sorry if I seem out of sorts.* But I couldn't forget—even if I wanted to—that we were friends. I owed her—and me—the truth.

"I'm not mad at you," I said. "Not *really.*"

"Not really, but sort of?" Jura asked.

I sighed. "I *was* mad. Still am, but . . ." I tried to think of a way to say it. "It's no one thing I'm mad at. It's everything! I fetched a bunch of wishes for a bunch of folks, and my gram still died."

"I can see that. Being mad," she agreed.

"So I did the one unforgivable thing." I turned away from the door and leaned my back against the library wall. "I broke the first rule. I made a wish *for myself.* Actually, I made a mess of wishes. Big ones. And now . . . I can't fetch wishes at all." I looked away from her. I didn't want to watch her face as she realized I wasn't good for much of anything anymore.

"Oh, Genuine."

"What?" I bumped my toes on the sidewalk. The sole of my shoe had started peeling away. *Ain't that fittin'?* I thought.

"I'm so sorry."

"Why?" I snapped. "'Cause I can't wish you up the perfect wedding dress for when you marry Sonny?"

"No, you clabberhead." She gave a somber little laugh. "Because that was the last thing your gram gave you, and now it's gone."

I very nearly went on the offensive. *Who are you calling a clabberhead?* But her words started to sink in, and I realized she was right. Gram had set that wish cup in my hands for the first time. Gram had taught me to draw down the starlight. Now Gram was gone. The cup was empty.

And I had no way to fill it up again.

My knees shook and my hands shook and even my lips and the very skin of my face shook from the inside, as if something sick was trying to get out.

I wept.

"Oh, God, Jura," I managed between gasps. "It's gone. I threw it away. Oh God, oh God, oh God." And then it struck me—the most despisable thing of all. "Jura! All those hungry people! No more wishes, no more biscuits. They're gonna starve!" I let out a moan from the deepest, hurtingest part of me.

I fell onto Jura and cried so hard that the whole shoulder of her sweater turned wet. She hugged me tight and stroked my hair in a way that reminded me of Gram, which made me bawl all the more. My whole world ended right there in Jura's kind arms, if you can make any sense of that. When I finally pulled away from her, I felt clean but raw, as if I'd been roughly scrubbed inside and out.

"Thanks," I said.

"Sure." She tucked a bit of hair behind my ear.

"Travis might be moving to California." It was a funny thing, I know, how that came to mind right then, but there it was.

Her eyebrows shot up. "How come?"

I told her about Travis's pa and Miz Tromp's quandary. "It's a right fine mess, that's all."

"You know, I bet we can fix it," Jura said after a time.

"How?"

"We could . . . get Travis's dad a job in town!"

"Because Sass is just brimming over with jobs?" I teased.

She paused. "Okay, no. But how about if—what if we applied for some kind of grant? For Wish to End Hunger? And then we could hire—what's his dad's name?"

"Kip."

"We could hire Kip to do all the mailing and stuff. Make him our office manager!" She looked at me with big, excited eyes.

"Jura."

"Yeah?"

"Wish to End Hunger is done. I'm wishless. Useless." My throat went tight. "Good for nothin' but scrubbing floors."

Jura jerked her chin back. "Genuine!"

"What?" I asked. "It's true. I'm nothing but Dangerous Dale Sweet's shine-less, free-lunch daughter."

She poked me on the shoulder. "Quit that! I mean it! You may be wishless, but you are *not* shine-less! I can't even count the number of people in this town you've helped—"

I cut in, "With *wishes*."

Jura set her hands firm on her hips. "When biscuit

numbers were running thin, did you tell people in need, *Good luck with that, Genuine's off the clock?* No! You figured out the whole Sass barter thing—neighbors helping neighbors. That's what you do! You help! You care! There is nothing *useless* about that!"

I was about to deny it. But just then, ever so faintly, in one lone corner of my mind, a few shimmering notes rang out. I could have sworn silver light flashed in the glass of a nearby windshield.

"Hey, uh . . . Jura?"

"Stop arguing with me! I'm—"

"I ain't arguing," I told her.

"You ain't?" She paused. "You're not?"

"No. Hold up." I waited to see if the notes would sound again.

They did.

I know it might have only been a wish that I'd heard it, or a memory of a song I'd known before. But I let it speak to me. And finally, I thought I was starting to understand. *All shall be well.*

I reached out and squeezed my friend's hand. "You're right kind, Jura, and I thank you. But hush, now. I've got an idea. We've got to get back to work. Wish to End Hunger might not have to close up shop after all."

* * *

We called it the Sass Unstoppable Barter Alliance, and it was a way for poor and hungry folks to do for themselves when no one else could — or would — help them.

"Like Cornucopio," Jura said, making herself comfortable in the library chair. "But more . . . Genuine."

Jura set us up a website where people could volunteer as scouts, as we called 'em. The scouts would go into their towns and start making lists — just like Jura and I had done in Sass. Who had what, who needed what. Then, the volunteers would post their lists at the SUBA site. On our end, Jura and I would watch for "needs" that couldn't be met locally and start pairing them up with far-off "haves" — farmers with surplus food crops, for instance. The "haves" would have "needs," too, so everyone got something, and no one felt less-than. It would be tricky, we figured, sometimes rassling the lists of three and four communities to make sure everyone's haves and needs got met, but with Jura's computer smarts, we'd soon have a fancy math formula that would do most of the work for us. Much easier than baking biscuits till four in the morning!

"The main thing is, how do we get a bunch of corn from Pitney, Georgia, all the way to, say, Sydney, Australia?" I asked. "Shipping things that won't fit in the mail. That's gonna be the hard part."

"Don't forget, Genuine, you're a newsmaker!" Jura

walked past the dispatch desk and snatched up a *New York Times*. She flipped a few pages, then handed it to me.

There it was, right next to an article about unseasonable heavy rains in the South. GEORGIA GIRL GRANTS WISHES. It was a tiny speck of a thing, but maybe it would be enough.

Jura put on her best Sass accent. "We got to capitalize on all this media ruckus, little missy! Call up that-there Kathleen Kroeger and tell her to make herself useful!"

"That was terrible!" I laughed.

"Turrible accent," she agreed, "but a mighty fine notion." Switching back to citified Jura, she added, sifting through her satchel, "When we get your message out, people will be lining up to help. Here. I think I've got Kroeger's number written in my—Yes, here. Call her."

I gritted my teeth at the thought of another meeting with Kathleen Kroeger, but in the end, it turned out not to be so bad. We held the interview in front of the school, so I was dressed in regular clothes and ol' Drunken Dale was nowhere in sight. Miz Kroeger was eager to help us promote anything that might bring her the "international audience" she was "born to reach." Plus, the newswoman was so enchanted by Scree Hopkins—who'd been lured by all the cameras—that she hired Scree on the spot as her rural correspondent and intern.

21

A GENUINE SWEET

JURA AND I WERE PUZZLING OUT THE WHATS AND wherefores of SUBA till nearly nine. We knew we were onto something good, and might have even kept on till ten, had the weather not started to turn sour.

It began with a howling wind—and I mean that. If you've never heard a wind howl, you may think it's a figure of speech, but it ain't. It didn't take more than a few noisy gusts to convince us we had to head home.

By the time we were halfway along Main Street, the rain was pelting down. It was a sudden, heavy storm, with sharp drops that felt like little needles on the skin.

"We can't walk home in this!" Jura shouted over the din.

"Maybe Ham will give us a ride. He's just closing." I began splashing my way across the street. The sock in my sole-broken shoe turned instantly soggy.

Ham's door was locked, but our frantic knocking brought him out of the kitchen. He squinted at us through the door, saw who we were, and let us in.

"Creation! Get in here!"

We hurried inside.

"Can you give us a ride home, Ham?" I asked, dripping all over his freshly mopped floor.

He nodded. "Gimme two shakes. I was just locking up. Y'all grab yourselves an apple fritter."

A few minutes later, Jura and I squeezed into the cab of Ham's truck.

"I don't know if your daddy's apt to be home, Genuine," Ham said as we drove. That was his nice way of saying, *Your daddy could be dead drunk, anywhere.* "I don't like the thought of you alone in all this weather. Think your ma would mind if Genuine spent the night, Jura?"

Jura said she was sure her ma and her auntie would be fine with that.

We pulled up to Jura's house. A face appeared in the window and disappeared. A few seconds later, Miz Carver—who was as tall and round as Jura was petite and lean—appeared on the porch, opened an umbrella, and ran out to greet us.

"Thanks, Ham!" She waited for us to climb out, then waved Ham away with a friendly, "Now, go home! Before you have to swim there!" As she escorted us to the house, she poked each of us in turn. "Where have you been? You don't call your mama when you're running late?"

Inside, we started peeling off our wet clothes.

Miz Carver handed us towels for our hair. "Go upstairs and put some dry things on. You are staying the night, aren't you, Genuine?"

"Yes, ma'am. If you don't mind."

She laughed. "Mind? You two have been joined at the hip for a month, and I haven't even had a chance to show you my collection of Fisk fuel extraction converters!"

"Mom!" Jura protested.

"I'm joking!" Miz Carver replied. "Unless you *want* to see them, Genuine?"

"Mom!"

"You don't know what you're *miss*-ing," Jura's ma sang. "Fine. Go change. And hurry. A glass of warm milk and then it's off to bed with you. It's already—" She glanced at the clock. "Lordy, it's already past ten!"

Miz Carver tucked Jura and me into her big bed and kindly said she'd take the foldout sofa downstairs. Jura's auntie Trish said she'd hear none of *that*—that we girls couldn't have all the fun of a slumber party and leave the women out. Aunt Trish promptly grabbed an armful of pillows and blankets and joined Miz Carver on the sofa bed.

We could hear their glad, sisterly chatter between the breaks in the wind—till we fell asleep, at least.

Thanks to the rough weather the next morning, TV reception was reduced to pure static. The radio was clear enough, though: school had been canceled on account of rain. Government offices were closed and so was Ham's, the grocery, and every other business in town. Every thinking person should stay in, because a number of the main roads were flooded and more rain was on the way.

"Does this happen a lot?" Jura asked me while us four women sat around the radio with blankets snug on our shoulders.

"Hardly ever," I told her. "But then, our autumns aren't usually as wet as this one, either. The only other time I remember, I was real small. I think some of the low-lying houses got evacuated."

"Are we low-lying?" Miz Carver asked her sister.

"Not especially," Jura's auntie replied. "I don't think."

Jura and I exchanged a worried glance.

By two that afternoon, the winds had picked up again and the electric went out. We found some batteries for the radio, but the DJ said he may not be broadcasting for much longer. The station's generator was hiccoughing and the backup broke last winter.

"If you're out there, Genuine Sweet," the DJ joked, "wish me up some repairs!"

* * *

It was nearly six p.m., and the rain still hadn't stopped. The water had crept up to the front door, and the house began to smell of damp.

"What should we do?" Jura wondered aloud.

"Don't suppose you can wish the rain away?" Miz Carver asked me.

"No, ma'am," I replied. "Sorry."

We didn't sleep at all that night. The ceiling sprang a leak, and despite the caterwauling of the rain and wind, it was the dripping sound that kept us up.

The only food we had left was salty canned or salty bagged. The tap water was contaminated from the storm, and we didn't have any electricity to boil it. We were thirsty.

Still the rain went on.

Around eight the next morning, a boat floated up to the house. It was Ham and his dog, Meaty, who greeted us gladly, his pink tongue a-flopping.

"Lotta rain!" Ham shouted. "We're all of us gathering at the Community Center. They got generators and food, and a whole mess of bottled water."

Jura and me climbed in first, then Miz Carver and her sister.

It took nearly an hour to row to the Community Center. It sat on the tallest hill in town—and even *its* parking lot was a little flooded. The rain, for now, was only a drizzle, but more fat, dark clouds loomed in the distance.

"It's got to stop sometime," Ham observed.

We clambered from the boat and half walked, half climbed to a dry spot on the hill. Through the windows of the building, we could see lights on inside. I couldn't help sighing my relief. Just seeing those lights after so long without electricity was proof, somehow, that something normal still existed in the world.

It was a strange thing to see pretty much everyone I knew sitting around on cots, every one of us greasy-haired and smelly from worry and lack of clean water.

It was even stranger to see the hope bloom on their faces when I arrived.

"It's Genuine!" someone whispered.

"Thank goodness!" another someone replied.

People stood up. They smiled. They gathered 'round.

You know what they wanted, of course. They wanted me to wish away the storm.

"Leave her be," Ham shouted. "She's tired like the rest of you. She'll get to it when she's good and ready."

"Our houses'll float away if she waits too long," someone said.

"She can rest after she wishes all this water away." It was Chickenlady Snopes.

"Please—" I said softly to Ham.

He looked down at me.

"I can't," I told him.

"That's what I said," he spoke to me, but loudly enough for other folks to hear. "Too tired to wish anything right now. Of course you are."

"No. Ham." I tugged on his sleeve. "I really can't. The magic's gone."

He looked at me as if my words didn't make sense. "For real?"

I nodded.

"Dang." He deflated before my eyes.

I nodded again.

The voices around us grew louder and keener — some of them angry, even. Why hadn't I fixed the flooding already? Didn't I know people was losing their homes? Fairly irresponsible of me to let things get this far out of hand. Guess I took after my pa after all — born tired and raised lazy.

They crowded around me. They made faces and pointed fingers. They were, all of them, full-grown tall, and I was feeling mighty overwhelmed.

"Hey!" a voice called.

Like a school of guppies, everyone turned at once.

Travis stood on top of a crate of canned peas, waving his arms wildly. "Quit your bellyachin' and back the blazes off!"

When they saw it was Travis, most folks turned my way again and carried on with their complaining.

Travis wasn't deterred. "Hello! Stupid people of Sass!"

That got their attention.

"Y'all seem to think this girl owes you something!" he shouted.

"Them what has, does," Jerry Tatum shouted in reply.

"I think you mean, them what has, *gets*, Jerry," Travis called back. "As in, them what *has* a lick of sense *gets* off their butts and solves their own problems." He folded his arms over his chest. "Do you realize you're expecting a twelve-year-old kid to save you from an act of nature? Now, I know as well as anyone that Genuine is a magical girl." He met my eyes and nodded. "But is it fair—or even moral—to lay your troubles at her feet? In *this* town, of all places?"

"Heck, yeah!" Ruby Hughes hollered unprettily. "All she has to do is snap her fingers and the storm's gone! You think we can do *that* for ourselves?"

Ruby glared at me, full of hate. I couldn't help thinking back to the day in the girls' bathroom, when she'd gotten so mad because I wouldn't wish up her horse tack. *Any fool can wish on a stupid star,* she'd said. Ruby had been spouting nonsense out of anger and spite, but . . .

Any fool can wish on a stupid star.

Huh.

Following Travis's example, I grabbed a chair and stood on it. "Maybe you can! Have you tried?"

"We ain't no wish fetchers!" Dirk Yardley shouted.

I was running out of patience. Did I mention? It really clumps my grits when people give up easy.

"How do you know?" I called back.

Oh, they didn't like that at all. There was grumbling and griping, and I think someone even spit.

Sheriff Thrasher appeared at my side. He had his hands on his belt and a no-nonsense look on his face. "That's enough, now, Genuine. It's time to wish the flood away."

"I'm sorry, sir," I said, still on top of the chair. "I really can't. I broke the wish fetcher's first rule, and now my magic's gone."

Somebody threw a balled-up piece of paper at me. Travis was off his crate in a flash, making his way through the crowd toward me.

Meanwhile, I heard somebody say, "Arrest her, Sheriff!"

A choir of other voices agreed.

Sheriff Thrasher looked one way and then the other, like he was thinking it over. "All right, Genuine, I can see you need some time to get back to right thinking." Turning his eye toward the rumbling posse, he added, "And these folks need some time to cool off. Let's go."

"You're joking, Mike!" Ham exclaimed.

"Take your hands off her, you cull!" Travis shouted.

Suddenly, I was struck with the silliness of the situation.

I laughed. "You can't honestly mean to *row* me to the jail, Sheriff?"

The sheriff tugged me away from the throng to a gray door that said STAFF. Somebody had stuck a little yellow piece of notepaper to it that read *Jail*.

"It's for your own good, girl. Git." Sheriff Thrasher opened the door, nudged me into what was plainly a broom closet, and locked the door behind me.

"Hey! You can't do this!" I banged on the door. "Let me out!"

"Shhut!" said a groggy voice from behind me.

I turned around.

Pa sat on an upturned bucket, one eye open. I guess even he couldn't sleep through all my racket.

"You." I narrowed my eyes.

He nodded. "Gen'wine."

I sighed.

"You don't say 'lo to your pap?" he slurred.

"'Lo," I snarled back.

"Heh, heh. She's a gen'wine Sweet after all, in jail with her pap. Like father, like daughter." He shook his head with mock pride.

I tried to ignore him and went back to banging on the door. "Sheriff Thrasher! You open this door right now!"

"Hey, hey, m'head hurts!" Pa protested.

I spun like a flash. "Don't you dare complain! Don't you dare! Do you even *know* Gram's dead?"

He jerked his head back and regarded me.

"Shore I do," he replied, rubbing a hand across his eyebrows. "Took her to the hospital, didn't I?"

"*You* took her to the hospital." I didn't believe it.

"Who else?"

"Drunk and dangerous Dale Sweet, if-he-ain't-drinkin'-he's-passed-out Dale Sweet? *You* heard Gram calling for help and took her to the hospital?"

"She didn't call out," he told me. "She came to my door. Knocked."

I was all sarcasm when I said, "She was dying, but she knocked."

He nodded. "And I opened my eyes and there she was, standing over me."

"You lie," I told him.

"Not so, not so." He held up a hand, palm out. "She said to me, 'Lights are out, Dale. 'S time to go.' So I got up and grabbed m'keys and asked her where she wanted to go. 'Hospital,' she told me. And so I took her."

I would have turned the whole story aside as a fable had he not said, "Funny, how she looked all silver in the dark."

"Silver?"

He nodded. "I said, 'Ain't ever seen no angel before,' and

she laughed and said, 'You still ain't. Turn the key 'n' drive, Dale.' Tha's what she said." He chuckled. "M'hands was nearly froze. Feet, too. Cold night that night. Dang cold."

I was standing there, with my hand on that big, gray door, partly turned toward Pa and partly turned away.

"You might have froze to death yourself," I said.

"Naw. Drink enough'll keep a man warm. Heh, heh."

I let that pass. "What happened when you got to the hospital?"

He shrugged. "Some people come around, ask if we need help, whatnot. All o' th'sudden, Starla crumples like a empty can."

I can't say how, but I saw it right then, so clear in my mind's eye. Gram *had* just crumpled. Something had left her and she'd just crumpled. Her time had come. It wasn't the cold that had killed her, after all.

"Was she still silver?" I asked, though I thought I knew the answer.

"Naw. Jus' for that time she was walkin' around." Pa paused. "Weren't long after that, they put her in a bed and them machines went wild, beep-beepin'. They came and said she died." He rubbed his hand through his hair. "Gonna miss that old girl. She never judged me harsh. She never did."

I stood stock-still for a time, just watching that night play itself out like a movie in my head. By the time I was ready to ask Pa another question, he was passed out again.

I rolled my eyes. "Mighty nice talking to you."

But then, after a minute, I had to admit—it sort of had been.

I was asleep myself when I heard the door unlock. I opened my eyes in time to see the sheriff give me a stern look before he allowed Jura to shuffle by him. She had a plate in each hand. The door shut behind her.

"Mm-mmm! Room-temperature canned peas and beets!" she teased. "You hungry?"

I took the plates from her and set one beside Pa. "You in trouble, too?"

"No. I told Thrasher I might be able to talk some sense into you."

I sighed. "It don't matter how much sense you make, Jura. The magic's gone."

"No, no. I know," she said. "What I really wanted was to ask you something."

"What?"

She leaned her back against the door. "Did you mean what you said out there? About how people couldn't know for sure they couldn't fetch wishes because they'd never tried?"

It took me a second to even remember having said it. "Guess I must have."

"I was thinking—what if you teach someone else to fetch wishes?" Her eyes sparkled at the notion.

I quirked my lips. "I dunno. Maybe. You want me to try to teach you?" It did make some sense. If somebody else could grant wishes, *they* could fetch the flood away.

"No, Genuine." Jura smiled. "I want you to try to teach *everybody*."

22

YELLOW SHERBET SUNRISE

URPRISINGLY, THERE WEREN'T A LOT OF TAKERS. In the end, it was Jura and me, Dilly Barker, Travis and Miz Tromp, Ham, and Mister Strickland on top of that hill outside of town hall. Well, Sheriff Thrasher was there, too, but I think that was mostly to keep an eye on me.

It was full dark out, and each one of us had a plastic cup in hand. Problem was, the sky was blanketed with clouds and, yes, it was still raining.

"I don't know if this is going to work," I said to the others. "I think the best thing you can do is imagine the stars on the other side of the clouds. Really see them as best you can. Then, once you have them clear in mind, whistle."

"Whistle how?" Dilly Barker asked.

"Loud and firm," I replied.

"Like you're callin' a pig?" Ham asked.

"Something like that," I agreed.

They started whistling.

"Wait!" I shouted. "Sorry. Hold up your cups, too. All right. Now, just call the starlight down, if you can."

They each had their way of doing it. Jura held her cup in one hand, and as she whistled, she gestured a welcome with the other. Ham did indeed whistle like he was calling his prize pig. Meanwhile, he shoved the cup at the sky like he was offering the stars a pail of sweet feed. Mister Strickland's whistles came short and fast, and he tapped the bottom of the cup as he went. Miz Tromp's crooning was soft and sweet, and Dilly Barker's made me think of fairy tales, for some reason.

Travis held his cup in both hands and pressed it hard to his forehead. He stayed like that for a long time, real still, before he began to whistle. It started out as a low, spreading sound, if that makes sense to you, but all at once, it became a tune—one I'd heard before.

It was the song the stars sang.

It was then, when Travis's song streamed into the night, that the clouds gave way and the starlight began to flow.

"If that don't beat all," Sheriff Thrasher whispered.

I don't think the others even heard him, they were so astonished by the six quicksilver waterfalls that spilled from the sky into their cups and over their hands, splashing to the ground, casting flares of silver sparks that danced like brief fireflies in the night.

When the cascade stopped, Travis turned to me, his hands dripping starlight. His breath was short, like he'd just run a race, and he was grinning so hard you'd have thought he was another Travis entirely. "What do we do now?"

The others looked up, also waiting for my answer.

I told them about how my great-gram drank the starlight, and how Gram used her pocket lint to make wish seeds from it. "And y'all know about my wish biscuits," I said. "I guess I'll tell you what Gram told me. It's best if you find your own way."

There came a long period of quiet then, while the new wish fetchers considered the method that might be their own. In the end, not every one of them decided right then, but here's what each of them finally concluded.

Instead of wish biscuits, Miz Tromp makes beautifully iced wish cupcakes. I myself have been the recipient of a Miz Tromp wish, and it's no fable to say those cakes taste like sunshine drenched in honey.

Ham pours his starlight into the gas tank of his truck, and then, something like a magical compass, the truck nudges him wherever he needs to go to find the substance of a person's wish.

Dilly Barker dips her fingertips in the starlight and

smudges a few drops of it between the eyebrows of anyone who has need of a little enchantment.

Mister Strickland lets his chalk soak overnight in the silvery stuff, and anytime someone has a good-hearted wish, he writes it out ten times on a special chalkboard he reserves for just that purpose.

At first, Jura mixed hers with soap and blew wish bubbles. Lately, though, she's taken to hopping buses to new towns and secretly dumping pure starlight into their water supply.

As for Travis, he uses his to fill the shafts of ink pens. Anytime he meets someone who's unhappy, he gives them a pen. "Write your own story," he tells them, "with you as the hero. Give yourself a happy beginning, middle, and end."

It was Dilly Barker who went to Sheriff Thrasher that night and asked for his wish.

"Uh, I, uh, I hardly know," he said. I think he was still sort of stunned from the whole parting-of-the-clouds, downpour-of-starlight thing.

Ham walked up behind the cop and cleared his throat. "I think earlier you mentioned something about the flooding, Mike."

"Oh! Right!" the sheriff said.

"Well, then," said Dilly. "Wish away, my fine fella."

So he did. And not a thing changed. Not that night,

anyway. It was drizzling as the eight of us trudged back through the mud into the town hall, and I could still hear the patter of the rain on the roof as I fell asleep in my cot.

Every citizen in Sass must have been standing on top of that hill that morning, looking down over our soggy city. Soggy, I say, but no longer flooded. The waters had receded, and although there was a fair amount of nature's flotsam collected along the curbs—tree branches and the like—the buildings looked downright sound. All the birds were chirping, and the sunrise painted the sky tangerine and yellow like the most beautiful sherbet you ever saw.

"The sun keeps on shinin' like that, things'll dry out in no time," Ham said. A mutter of general agreement passed before he added, "So. Who's gonna help me drag my boat home?"

At first, no one answered him. After the upscuddle last night—and the way the flood got fixed in spite of folks' hardness—I imagine my neighbors weren't feeling too proud of themselves.

Handyman Joe was the first to break the sheepish silence. "I've got a trailer on my truck. Won't take me but ten minutes to run home and get it."

"Think the church bus has enough seats to get these folks back to the seniors' home in one trip?" I heard Pastor Missy ask.

"We can get 'em there, but the whole place was flooded out, down to the last linen," someone replied.

"I can board two at my place," Missus Fuller called.

"So can I," said Miz B.

And so, real gradual but real steady, we started to get things back in order. Miz Tromp helped me and Jura organize the seventh-graders into a steam-cleaning, laundering power-house, all our supplies coming free of charge from Sass Foods.

One more thing happened before we all left the hill that morning.

I was unlocking the door to Pa's jail—he was still in there, still asleep, and muttering something about a note from Gram—when I felt a hand on my shoulder. I turned around. It was Dilly Barker, the lady who'd given me the miracle flour.

"Hey, Dilly," I said.

"Hey, Genuine. How are you?"

I thought about it. "I'm all right."

"Good, good." Dilly nodded. "Listen. I just wanted to say, I think it's only fair for me to give you something in exchange for those wish-fetching lessons."

"Oh, no," I replied. "You don't need to—"

"I do and I will." She said it sternly but she patted my arm. "Next weekend, I want you to come by my place, 'round about nine a.m., you hear? I'm gonna teach you how to mill flour."

Then she winked, smiled, and walked away.

23

THANKSGIVING

BY THE TIME THE SCHOOL BUILDING WAS DRIED out and cleaned, it was Thanksgiving break. With Gram gone and Pa, well, unchanged, I didn't have any particular plans of my own. Fortunately, I had good friends and a heap of invitations. Jura and I watched the Thanksgiving Day Parade on the library computer, and after that, we visited with Dilly, who greeted us at the door wearing a turkey-feather headdress. We played Chinese checkers and did a lot of laughing.

Later that afternoon, I parted ways with Jura. She was headed to the Wentz Family Annual Turkey Day Cookout, and I'd been invited to the Tromp place.

In case you're wondering, I hadn't spent a lot of time with Travis since the flood. Not because I didn't want to — or even because he didn't want to — but because he'd been in California with his pa. He'd only just come home. I couldn't help wondering if he'd made a decision, and if this would be the day I'd hear about it.

I found Travis on his bench swing reading a book.

"What you got there?" I called as I opened the gate.

"Book," he replied with a smile.

"I can see that, you clabberhead. Which one?"

"The Light in the Forest," he replied. "You read it?"

"Naw. Is it good?"

"Real good." He flop-eared the page he was on and shut the book. "I missed you."

"The same dog bit me." I smiled. I tried to keep on smiling as I asked, "Are you moving?"

He shrugged. "Thinkin' about it."

The feeling I had was something like being punched in the gut. I bet it was a full minute before I managed, "You like California?"

"It's different."

I nodded. "If you go, maybe I'll come visit you someday."

He set the book down on the swing, got up, and took my hand. "I'd like that."

In the kitchen, Miz Tromp managed a turkey, a big ol' smoked salmon, the baking of a pie, the icing of a cake, and the candying of at least twenty yams, and she did it all with the easy flair of a dancer.

"Hey, Miz Tromp," I greeted her. "Need any help?"

She dipped her finger in the gravy and tasted it. "I don't think so. Unless you two want to set the table."

We said we'd be glad to. Travis and I went to the cupboard, and he handed me off enough plates for five.

"You and me. Your ma. Tom. Who else is coming?" I asked him.

"My father," he replied. "He wanted to talk some stuff out with Ma."

Making plans for the big move, I reckoned.

I swallowed hard. "That's . . . um."

Travis spun on me and crossed his arms over his chest.

"That all you got to say about it? 'Um'?"

I couldn't tell if he was funnin' me or not.

Even if he was, I decided I didn't feel much like joking. "No. That's not all I have to say."

"Well, then?"

I stepped up and set my hands on my hips. "I don't want you to go. I don't think it's right. First, because I'm selfish, and I like having you around. But second, because I don't trust your pa. He left you all alone! And now, out of the blue, he turns up and wants to be your daddy? If you ask me, there's something rotten up that creek!"

"Who's your outspoken friend, Travis?" came a man's voice from behind me.

"This here's Genuine," Travis said. "Genuine, this is Kip. My father."

He was a beefy type, well-muscled and fit. His hair was cut short, and I could see where Travis got his big ears from.

"Something rotten up the creek, huh?" He reached out a hand to shake.

"Surely even you will admit the stench is a mite fishy, sir," I replied, though my voice shook a little.

He lowered his hand. "Fishy, because a man wants to know his boy?"

I stood my ground. "Fishy because he doesn't care whether he uproots his boy from a life he and his ma worked hard to build—without any help from that man, I'll add, when help was surely owed!" Warming to my subject, I pulled out my preaching finger. "Do you know they have a family business here? People rely on them for wedding cakes and skin smears and whatnot! They've got friends who care about them!"

"I can see that," Travis's pa replied.

But I wasn't done. "It's not fair what you're doing here, sir. And it's selfish. And if you're really trying to convince folks that you've changed, it's precisely this sort of selfishness you might want to take a gander at!"

"Is that so?" Kip asked.

"Yes, sir. It is." But my engine was running down. I was hearing my own words and thinking Kip *might* not be the only feckless father I was mad at. I dropped my arms to my sides and said a little more softly, "Now, I apologize if I've been rude, but sometimes a body's got to call it like they see it."

"Can't argue with that," he agreed. He raised an eyebrow in Travis's direction, then walked out.

Suddenly embarrassed, I set myself to folding Miz Tromp's dainty cloth napkins. When I finally looked up, Travis stared like he was seeing me for the first time.

"Sorry if I was outside my rights," I whispered.

He shook his head. "You wasn't."

"There's a tiny chance some of that upscuddle wasn't actually about you and your pa."

"Probably. But I'm still glad you said it."

As I set out Miz Tromp's good silver forks, I couldn't help noticing how fine they were, real ornate and heavy in the hand. Like the kind I imagined my great-great-gram might have had.

It had been a while since I'd thought about her. All at once, I couldn't help wondering if she and Gram, and Gram's ma and my ma, too, were all together somewhere. What would they be doing? What did dead wish fetchers do for fun?

Maybe, I thought, *they disguise themselves as stars and grant wishes.*

We sat down to eat around four. Things were a little uneasy to start, with Tom and Kip at the table, and at cross purposes. Miz Tromp was a fine hostess, though, and soon everyone was, well, politely unclenched. Plus, it turned out Kip was a jokester—his tales were real ripsnorters! All at once, it was plain where Travis got his hidden comedy streak. It was also plain why Travis might want to go to California.

And considering the way Miz Tromp looked at Tom while they talked herbal medicines and alternative treatment retreats, it was pretty easy to see why she was in so much agony over Travis's dilemma.

As for me, I knew I had to content myself with enjoying Travis's company now, for however long it lasted. Twice, while we ate, I poked Travis in the arm, just for the sake of feeling his warm skin under my fingertip. Both times, he didn't look up at me but caught my finger in the crook of his own and gave me a tug.

"I'd forgotten how small Sass was," Kip said at one point. "How many people in town?"

I was the only one who knew offhand. "Five hundred twenty-three last week. MaryLou Haines had twins."

"Do you know everyone by name?" he asked me.

"Just about," I replied. "A few folks like to keep to themselves."

"I've been wondering about those off-gridders, how they fared out there, with all the weather," said Miz Tromp.

All the weather was the name the town had unofficially agreed on for our overly wet fall and the recent unlikely pairing of snow and flood.

"They get radio, don't they?" Tom asked.

I nodded. "I think so."

"And TV, of course," said Kip.

Travis, Miz Tromp, and me laughed all at once.

"What did I say?" Kip asked, smiling good-naturedly.

"Nobody has TV," Travis said.

"Well, folks who have computers can get some of it," I clarified. "And we do have two channels, kind of. The cooking channel and the static news channel."

"The *static* news channel?" Kip echoed.

"Today in Washington—sssssssst," Travis mimicked, "a large pair of pants—sssssssst. In weather—sssssssst. A bear! Hahaha!"

"You're kidding." Kip was plainly horrified.

"If you want to learn to braise turnips, though, you're in the right place," I told him.

Kip shook his head as if our tale of woe had wounded his heart. It turned out he was some sort of media "seeding" guy. Which, if I understood it correctly, had something to do with planting big metal towers on pristine and scenic hills.

We ate until our buttons popped and then some. Before long, it was late enough to start heading to Ham's for the Cider Toast.

"So, the whole town gets together to drink cider?" Tom asked as we walked toward Main.

I shook my head. "Not just that. It's a Thanksgiving thing. You'll see."

Ham's doors were flung open, and the front walk was lined with tables. In great kegs, there was apple cider and peach cider and a new thing that year, blueberry. There was sugared cider—very, very sweet—and Granny Smith cider for the folks who preferred theirs sour. There was even spike cider, as they called it, though the grown folk were keeping a close eye on that table, so Travis and I didn't get a taste.

By the time the crowd finished gathering, it was dark and getting chilly. I wrapped my hands around my paper cup and breathed in the spiced steam as deep as I could.

"Let's get started!" Handyman Joe called. "There's a turkey sandwich calling my name."

"You can't possibly be hungry!" his wife replied.

"I'll go first," said Ham, clearing his throat. He held up his cup. "A toast! To the people of Sass. Neither snows nor floods shall keep us from the completion of our appointed, uh, turkey dinners."

A few folks groaned, but nearly everyone cheered before they drank.

When I saw Tom toss back his cider in a single throw, I warned him, "Best take that in sips, or you'll be up peein' all night."

He raised his eyebrows. "Ah."

"A toast!" shouted Dilly Barker. "To Starla MacIntyre Woods. She will be missed."

"Hear, hear," came several voices in reply.

"To Gram," I whispered. "And to Ma."

Travis heard, and clinked cups with me before he took an especially large swig.

Scree Hopkins waited the span of a whole two breaths before she cried, "A toast! To me and Micky Forks! We just got promised to be engaged!" She held up her hand and waved it wildly. I guess she must have had a ring on, but I couldn't see it.

An argument promptly started over in the Forkses' corner of things.

Sheriff Thrasher stepped up. "A toast! To a *peaceful* night. Right, folks?"

There was some shuffling and some elbow nudging, and the Forkses calmed right down.

"A toast! To our new crop of wish fetchers!" called Missus Fuller. "And to Genuine, who taught 'em!"

"To Genuine," a voice said softly in my ear. I turned to find Penny Walton standing there.

"Happy Thanksgiving, Miz Walton," I said. "How are you feeling?"

"Happy. Free." She took a deep breath of our country air. "Grateful to spend a holiday doing something besides worrying that it might be our last one together." She nodded in Edie's direction.

"I'm real glad for you," I said, and I meant it with all my heart.

She gripped my hand and squeezed it. "I'm sorry about your granny."

I gave her the brightest smile I could muster, hugged her, and watched as she drifted back to her kin.

Several swigs later, Kip asked me, "So, what's a wish fetcher?"

I started to tell him it weren't nothin' (I had learned my lesson about keeping certain things private, after all), but JoBeth Haines — pretty as a picture in a green and gold party dress — stepped into the circle and said, "A toast!" She pointed her cup in Kip's direction. "To new friends." Then she blushed. Furiously.

Kip's eyes got wide at the sight of the librarian/dispatcher, and I was surprised to see his cheeks flare red, too. A few seconds passed before he managed to smile, lift his cup, and return, "To new friends."

After that, Kip didn't care what a wish fetcher was. He and JoBeth floated together like magnetized motes of dust. Next thing I saw, they'd made their way to a nearby bench and — once the toasting was done — there we left them.

★ ★ ★

My house was empty when I got home. I wasn't surprised. Still, I left a plate of Miz Tromp's goodies beside Pa's bed before I went into Gram's room and shut the door behind me.

It was time, I'd decided earlier that day, to let some of her things go. There were all sorts of warm clothes in her closet, not to mention a whole chest of quilts that someone could make use of. I'd ask Jura to post them on the SUBA site.

Slowly, carefully, I took everything from its place and set it on the bed. I cried a little as I boxed up Gram's powders and such. I bawled like a baby when I folded her robe. In the end, I only kept three things. Gram's wish cup. A stack of letters — most of them from folks who'd contacted my ma for wishes, back when. And a framed photo of Gram and Ma and me, taken when I was nothing more than a bump in Ma's belly.

I moved back into Gram's room, my old room, that night.

The place seemed awful empty.

I dreamed of letters and notes, packages and papers. So many of them! Cascading down from the sky, flooding in through the windows. Some of it was my ma's old mail, but there were other things, too. I picked an envelope off the floor. It was addressed to me.

My eyes snapped open.

A note from Gram! Pa said something about a note from Gram!

In a flash, I was on my feet and tearing the house apart. I moved furniture and flung piles of Pa's dirty laundry. I spilled out drawers and even checked to see if a letter got stuck somehow to their undersides.

I went through every closet, every chest, every keepsake box. I even looked in the pockets of Gram's winter coat. Nothing. Heartsick, I flung myself onto the couch.

Something crunched beneath me.

Cushions flew. And there it was, wedged between the pillows! A carefully folded slip of paper with my name on it.

In Gram's wobbly but beautiful cursive, she had written this:

My Genuine Beauty Sweet,

How proud I was when I got your call tonight! This thing you're doing for Penny Walton — how gracefully you are coming into your own! You're a true MacIntyre woman and the sort of wish fetcher I always dreamed you would become.

Thank the stars, while I was busy being cautious and tight-lipped, you blossomed into a real courageous girl. One who does what's right, no matter what her fretful

old granny says. I reckon, in the end, you set a better
example for me than I did for you. I'm so pleased for
your mettle. You've taught me how to face providence
more bravely.

Now, if for some reason you don't see me as soon as
you might expect, don't you worry. Everything's taken
care of here, and I mean that. I AM ALL RIGHT. Your
only business is to be your beautiful self and, as I told
you once before, to find your own way. All shall be well.

I love you, Gen. So much.

I'll see you when I see you,

Your Gram

In a corner of the letter was a faint bit of silver where, I
imagined, Gram's hand had lingered.

My gram was all right.

24

RURAL NEWS NETWORK

A FEW MORNINGS LATER, I WAS ROUSED BY A KNOCK on the front door. It was Travis.

"Come on," he said.

"What? Is something wrong?"

"Just come on." He tugged at my arm.

It was so cold out, his words turned the air to smoke, so I left on my pajamas and put something more presentable over them. Then a coat. Then my boots.

"All right, now! What?" I demanded as I followed him out the door.

He grabbed me tight by the hand and led me downtown. When we got there, let me tell you, there was quite a hooray going on.

Penny Walton's car with the big WALTON REAL ESTATE magnets along the side sat parallel parked in front of two empty storefronts. Penny herself was looking a bit bedraggled, but she nodded eagerly as she sipped from a HAM's coffee mug, Travis's pa speaking, well, *at* her is the best way to describe it. JoBeth Haines stood at Kip's side, apparently explaining things when his communications lapsed into California-speak.

But that wasn't all. There were two TV vans and a whole mess of nicely dressed people milling about. They didn't look like they'd had any more sleep than Penny, but they bustled around with a great deal of purpose. They folded their arms and looked meaningfully at the storefront. They pointed at the wires overhead and the abandoned phone tower on Cheegee Hill. They stood on the roof of Ham's Diner, shouting into their cell phones and conversing with each other at the same time.

Tom's jeep was parked nearby, too. Him and Miz Tromp seemed to be walking in a big circle, right in the middle of the intersection of Main and Earl, talking something through. Sometimes he'd stop pacing and just turn around to look at her for a long time. Sometimes she'd grab him by the sleeve and wave her hands like she surrendered.

While Travis and I looked on, Mayor Cussler's pickup pulled up. He climbed out dressed in a suit and tie, which was startling, seeing as how I'd only ever seen him in jeans. He hightailed it over to Penny, JoBeth, and Kip.

"What on earth is all this?" I asked Travis.

"If everything goes well," he said, grinning, "you're witnessing the birth of the Rural News Network."

"What's that?"

"It's a scheme Kip made up—and I'm helping him," Travis replied. "A TV channel that gets picked up direct by special satellite receivers. Real news, no static. We aim to build one in every small town, everywhere. And the headquarters is gonna be right here, in Sass."

"That's *huge*," I said.

After my shock wore off, I realized: "That's jobs! Here in Sass!"

And another thing: "You're gonna stay! Doesn't that mean you're gonna stay?"

"Near as I can figure," he replied.

The Rural News Network. I shook my head. "I don't understand how it happened."

"You don't?" Travis pointed to Kip and JoBeth. They were standing awfully close, looking real cozy.

I couldn't help feeling a little aggrieved for Travis. The presence of his son, alone, wasn't enough to bring Kip to Sass, but just add a lady friend to it—

"It's all right," Travis said, as if he'd read my thoughts. "I'm figuring out who he is. I won't let him hurt me."

I wasn't sure it would be that simple, but I wished it were so with all my heart. And considering the smile on Travis's face as he eyed the commotion, I couldn't help being excited for him.

"So what about your ma and Tom?" I pointed to the two of them, still pacing in the street.

"Oh, he jumped the gun and said something about getting engaged," Travis said. "She told him he was addled, but she ain't exactly sent him away. I expect that's what they're bickering about now."

"Maybe he's in a rush 'cause he's afraid one of Kip's TV people is gonna snatch her up. Give your ma her own cooking show. Make her a star." I made little sparkle motions over my head.

Travis laughed.

I just stood there for a time, enjoying the look of him, of his smile.

"I am glad you're staying," I said at last.

Then he kissed me, all boyfriendly, but still real polite.

And *then* we went over to see what we could do to help fetch the Tromps' big wish.

25

SOMETHING LIKE A FAMILY

I RECKON WE'RE CLOSE TO THE END OF THE STORY — AT least the one you came to hear. As I said, I ain't fetching wishes no more. I don't know. Maybe I could if I really tried. Someday.

Happily, there's no shortage of wish fetchers in Sass now.

As for Travis — though he has his fits and starts — most days he leaves his surly black pants and his angry black shirt at home. He works afternoons at the RNN and is the youngest TV executive east of the Mississippi. Having something worthwhile to do with himself — not to mention, *ahem,* a girlfriend and a sideline fetching wishes — seems to suit him fine.

Jura and Sonny broke up the second week of December. It was a friendly sort of thing. Jura wanted to focus on SUBA and her college applications, and Sonny wanted to spend more time buddying up to Travis. I think he fancies himself a news anchor someday.

Tom's retreat center opened just last week. Penny Walton is his biggest investor, and Miz Tromp supplies all the herbal fixin's.

Tom and Miz Tromp are "seeing each other exclusively" (according to Miz Tromp), or they're "practically engaged" (according to Tom). Meanwhile, JoBeth Haines and Kip Tromp actually *are* engaged, set to be married this summer.

Pa still drinks too much. But he did get a part-time job sweeping floors at the RNN, so that's something.

Who else might you want to know about? Let's see. Scree Hopkins and Micky Forks tried to run off and elope a couple weeks ago. Micky leaves for military school next week.

So there you have it. Only two more scraps and we'll have a quilt.

Not long after Thanksgiving, I was by myself, reading, when a strange notion came to me. I simply *knew* I needed to take a walk.

It was cold out, of course, being December, so I put on my heavy coat and one of Gram's scarves—a handmade, shimmering white one that I'd always thought made her look so beautiful.

Seeing as how I was alone in the house, there wasn't anyone to say goodbye to on my way out.

I walked along the creek for a while, following it until it bent like a hairpin. There it met up with Deer Run Way, which took me toward town. It was a back road and a long-ish walk. I was a little lost in my thoughts when I suddenly found myself beside my favorite old tree, the one I reckoned had known my great-great-gram so well.

I found a patch of sunlight beneath and was just about to take a seat on the ground when I heard a voice calling my name. I looked up to find JoBeth Haines waving at me from the police station/library.

"Genuine! You got to see this!" she hollered.

A bit regretfully, I got up and headed her way. I'd been looking forward to some quality time with my kin, even if it was only in my imagination.

Holding the door open for me, JoBeth said, "I'm so glad I saw you there! You won't believe it!"

"What is it?" I asked, only a little curious.

She pulled a magazine from behind the counter. "It's the new *Georgia History Today*! It just came in!"

As a rule, I do enjoy a good *Georgia History Today*, but it wasn't until I saw one of the articles listed on the cover that my heart gave a little flutter. "The Georgia MacIntyres: Wishing on a Star," it said.

"What on earth — ?" I asked, already turning the pages.

"Read it!" JoBeth urged me.

I won't repeat the article word for word, but, boiled down,

here's what it said. Back in 1879, a Georgia astronomer by the name of Charlotte MacIntyre picked up a peculiar vibration on one of her instruments. She'd found a clump of stars that seemed to sing.

"Turn the page!" JoBeth said. "There's more!"

Not long after Charlotte had discovered the MacIntyre Cluster — which is what she called it — her daughter Stella started granting wishes, crediting the stars with her power. In time, Stella became so famous that President Theodore Roosevelt called her to the White House to fetch him a wish.

It hardly seemed possible! One of my own relatives fetched a wish for a U.S. president? My mind boggled at the very notion!

"If that don't take the whole biscuit!" I whispered.

"MacIntyre was your grandma's maiden name, wasn't it?" JoBeth asked.

I told her it was.

"You really should keep this, then." She tapped the magazine. "A nice reminder of her, maybe."

I said it was, and thanked her sincerely.

As I was leaving, JoBeth said to me, "You sure do have an extraordinary family, Genuine Sweet!"

An extraordinary family, I repeated to myself.

I nodded. "I reckon I do."

With the magazine tucked snug under my arm, I went back home. Pa was passed out on the sofa. Even in my room with the door shut, I could hear his snoring.

It was a pretty, snowy Christmas holiday, and I spent it warm, thanks to a new program Penny Walton helped Jura and me get started at the electric company. The Empowerment Partnership, it was called. The "partners" were Rumpp County Power, SUBA, and everyone Penny could pester into joining. Once a month we all got together to find ways to make sure everyone's electric bill got paid, whether they had the money or not. Sometimes we arranged work-for-power trades, other times we found donors. It wasn't always easy, but it was a real comfort to know that nobody in Sass would ever go cold again.

Christmas-wise, I received more than my share of invitations to parties and dinners. And never in all my born days had I gotten so many presents! Even after I'd failed to make all the weather go away, I guess a number of people still looked on me kindly.

But gifts and invitations—and even good friends like Jura and Travis—didn't make up for the fact that, when I came home at night, the place was usually empty. Even when Pa was there—well, you know—he wasn't much in the way of company. In short, I was lonely for kin.

* * *

That Christmas Eve, Miz Tromp and I sat together on the bench swing in front of her place. Travis and Tom and Kip were inside watching a football game — the RNN's first official broadcast.

"Ready for more marshmallows in that cocoa, Gen?" Miz Tromp asked me.

I liked how she'd taken to calling me Gen. It reminded me of Gram.

"Naw," I said, fiddling with my ma's old star necklace. I'd been wearing it a lot lately. "One more and it won't be cocoa anymore, it'll be marshmallow stew."

"Oooh! Now *there's* an idea," she said, ever the chef.

On the eaves overhead, the Tromps' Christmas lights blinked red-green-white in turn. I watched them for a time, thinking on how I'd never had any Christmas decorations at my house at all, until Gram had moved in and brought hers with her. I hadn't bothered to unpack them this year, though.

"Miz Tromp?" I said softly.

She sipped her cocoa. "Mm?"

"I was wondering, would you fetch me a wish?"

Her eyes got wide and she sat up very straight. "Course I would! Happy to! What for?"

"I don't know, exactly. I guess I'm tired of going home to a vacant house. It's nice of you and the Carvers to have me over all the time, but I miss my gram, and even though

I never met her, I miss my ma." I laughed. "In a way, I even miss my pa, because part of me can imagine what it might be like if he were, well, you know, really like a pa." I shook my head. "Maybe you can help with the phrasing of it, but I think my wish is for something like a family."

She set her cocoa on the porch rail and stood up. "All right."

"All right?" I asked.

"I just happen to have a wish cupcake tucked away for emergencies like this one."

"It's not really an emergency—" I started to say.

"Sure it is. Now come inside and don't argue."

What was I to do but follow?

I went inside, ate my cupcake—*Oh, Lordy, that melt-in-the-mouth cupcake!*—and after we talked for a while longer, I went home.

26

HOES AND ROWS

S O THERE YOU HAVE IT. GENUINE SWEET, TWELVE-YEAR-old wish fetcher, retired. Or, retired-ish, anyway.

It's a funny thing, isn't it, how a gift comes to a body? *Ping!* You're a wish fetcher! Here's your heavy yoke and more than a few sleepless nights! Maybe that's why, that night on the hill, only a very few people cared to learn to fetch wishes for themselves. They sensed that, in some ways, being a wish fetcher is harder than it is easy. Though I think there were probably other reasons, too.

Love does not triumph easily or without pain. A lady writer said that, and I think it's true. Wish fetching, when it's done right, has a lot to do with love. Not just loving people, but also loving life in all its sorrows and celebrations. When we see someone suffering and our gut urge is to reach out a hand rather than tearing off in the other direction, that's when we're ready, I think, to *really* start fetching wishes.

You might be wondering why I'm saying this to you. Well, I heard that Dilly Barker taught her schoolteacher cousin, Shevonne, to fetch wishes. Not long after, Miss Shevonne gave the gift to thirteen sixth-graders!

And, as you might imagine, I can't help worrying a little. Even if each of them kids only taught *one* person, and *those* fetchers taught one, and *those* fetchers ... It could be the second coming of the fall of the great city of Fenn.

But I do like to think better of people. Take you and me, for instance. Here we are, me talking till I hardly have any words left, and you listening for all you're worth. Thank you kindly for that, by the by.

Now you know my story. The ups, the downs, the shiny, and the grimy.

So if the gift comes your way—and there's a good chance it might—I know you'll remember. You'll think on star song and Cornucopio and all the weather. You'll recall the way the right wish can raise a smile, and how there are some troubles wishing can't fix. But most of all, I hope you'll remember what Gram said about finding your own way. Even if I never fetch another wish, even if no fetcher teacher ever appears in your town, there's nothing in the whole world—except our own selves—that can keep us from our good.

That's what I've learned, at least.

That, and how to mill some downright magical flour.